Home

M.L. GALLAGHER

Copyright © 2018 M.L. Gallagher
All rights reserved
First Edition

PAGE PUBLISHING, INC.
New York, NY

First originally published by Page Publishing, Inc. 2018

ISBN 978-1-64298-348-7 (Paperback)
ISBN 978-1-64298-349-4 (Digital)

Printed in the United States of America

PROLOGUE

Jason sat on the hillside opposite his cabin. He watched as the man came out of the slated rough-cut door, jumped off the porch, and walked up the path to the right of the cabin. He disappeared into the smaller cubicle to take care of his morning needs. When he emerged, he was still wearing the same huge grin that he had on his face when he hopped off the porch. Jason lowered his rifle and, looking down the sights, thought, *I bet if I put a bullet through your right eye, it would wipe that smile off your face.*

Just then the cabin door opened a second time, and Carey emerged carrying a bucket of water; she slung the contents off into the yard, and a female dog and three ragged puppies crawled out from under the house. She greeted each of them by name and squatted down to rub the dog's head. There was a sadness about her that Jason felt more than he saw. He lowered the rifle.

Carey stood up and, turning toward the barn, yelled, "Aren't you done yet? Breakfast is ready. It can't take long to feed one horse and five chickens. Hurry. It'll be cold." When she turned with her profile to Jason, showing her protruding belly, he raised the rifle and thought, *That little bastard will die too.*

CHAPTER ONE

Carey and Jason

When the war came, Carey and Jason had just put the finishing touches on their cabin. They had toiled together even before their marriage so that their little home in the hillside cove would be complete when they moved in. Carey prayed nightly that the western Virginia boys would not heed the news of war that was creeping through the mountains slowly, but eventually Jason and Carey were told that all the able-bodied men were expected to join.

Following John Brown's raid on the United States Arsenal and Armory at Harpers Ferry and his subsequent hanging, even the mountain residents were discussing the political ramifications. When the delegates sat down at the Virginia Convention of 1861, they would choose sides. In May, not quite a month after Virginia seceded, Jason's friend Daniel stopped in to visit at the Emerson cabin.

"Come on, Jason. Come with us," Daniel was saying as Carey came back in from feeding the dogs.

"Where do you want him to go?" she asked.

"It's a rally in Pruntytown to recruit forces for the Union cause."

Carey looked at Jason and ran back outside. Leaning against a pole that supported the roof of the porch that she and Jason had built side by side, she felt her anger build. He had promised her he would not even consider leaving to serve until there was no choice. She heard a noise behind her and turned to see Jason standing at the open door.

"Are you going with Daniel?" she demanded.

"Carey, it's just a rally."

"It's not just a rally. It's a recruiting rally. You know, rabble-rousing, joining up, marching off to war. If you go now, don't come back," she yelled, jumped off the porch, and started running across the meadow toward the creek.

Jason called out to her, but when she kept running, he thought it best if he let her cool off while he got rid of Daniel. When he stepped back inside, Daniel said, "She seemed a little bit upset."

"She's a lot upset, you moron. You knew I never planned on going to the rally."

"I can't believe you're letting her hold you back. Can you explain it?"

"I spent my entire life to get to this place. Carey and I have plans to start a family."

"You're dreaming. The country is at war."

"You go to your rally. I'm going to wait. Maybe I'll get lucky."

"You'll still have to go sooner or later. You know that."

"Yes, I know, but Carey has to be the reason I go, and right now she is the reason I can't go."

The wedding that Carey and her mother had been slowly preparing for would have to be rushed if the young couple would get the opportunity to spend their wedding night in the newly completed one-room cabin. The location of their cabin had been decided on when they were children running loose in the woods. Carey was eight and Jason was ten when they happened onto the cove. Even at that tender age, they already knew they would be together forever. Carey's grandmother, who was believed to be a wise woman by most and a witch by some, had told Carey and Jason that their destinies were entwined and nothing would make it different.

The cove was one of those places hidden in the deep woods. If you weren't paying close attention, you would pass right by without seeing the grassy meadow nestled between two mountain slopes. The creek that meandered through was a deep gully; the bushes and wildflowers growing along the edges obscured it from view. If you sat very still and listened, the faintest babble could be heard. Jason and Carey discovered it just that way, lying side by side on the hill, staring into each other's eyes.

Jason suddenly sat up and said, "Do you hear that?"

"What?" Carey said, sitting up beside him.

"There's water! I can hear it. This has always been our place. Now it can be our home. Come on!" He jumped up and started down the side of the mountain, which was no easy feat. It was steep, and he wasn't following any kind of path. Carey followed carefully, avoiding the low branches of the young poplar trees that dotted the hillside. Jason had completely disappeared from sight.

She called to him, "Wait up. Where are you?"

From behind a rhododendron thicket, she heard his voice.

"Just through the thicket. Be careful. The creek is surprisingly deep banked—" He didn't get a chance to finish his explanation before Carey slid through the last of the vinery and down the bank into the water. He couldn't help but laugh at her expression. The shock of the cold water made her grimace as she tried to catch her breath.

"I tried to warn you, but as usual, you had to find out for yourself," he commented with another laugh.

"So you think it's funny, do you?" Carey exclaimed as she asked for his assistance out of her predicament. Jason reached for her hand. The minute their hands touched, Carey pulled backward, and he was propelled into the creek face-first. They charged up and down the creek, laughing and kicking water on each other.

Jason helped Carey out of the creek and started rambling on about what kind of cabin they would build. He walked in a straight line from the creek bed to an old sycamore tree; its trunk was so big that it would have taken five grown men to reach around it. He pulled out his knife and began to carve his initials and then Carey's.

"After we are married, I will add a letter to show that we are together forever."

"Everyone already knows we will be together forever," Carey said, squeezing his hand.

The creek and the two hillsides became their place. They would agree to meet each afternoon when chores were done. Carey would come from her folks' house and wait on the side of the mountain until Jason would arrive on the opposite hillside. They found two resting spots halfway up the side where they could look across at each other and down onto the future cabin site. After a time, they would climb down to the creek bed and, knee deep in the cold water, share a passionate kiss. By this time, Carey was almost sixteen; it was becoming progressively harder to honor her promise to her mother concerning sex, but she was determined to have a wedding that did not involve a shotgun. She knew this was a burden for Jason, but his love kept him strong, and she knew he would wait.

When the War Between the States caused the acceleration of the wedding plans, Jason thought it was a blessing. All the young men were excited about going to fight; no one believed the conflict would last very long. Carey and most of the mothers and daughters were not convinced.

Then word that a Grafton guard member had been killed on the road near the Fetterman Bridge reached the mountain cove. They were leaving the rally that Daniel had invited Jason to when they heard, "Halt." Daniel had looked around. He heard the sharp report of a pistol, Daniel heard a crack, and Bailey lay dying on his back in the road. Daniel jumped down the bank and dove into the river. He stayed as low in the water as possible and floated downriver. Unfortunately, he climbed out of the river into the midst of a Confederate camp; he was mistaken as a recruit and found himself enlisting in the Confederate army. He marched off to Philippi sixteen miles south of where his buddy Bailey fell to fight in the first land battle of the War Between the States. By the time word of the battle at Philippi reached the mountain, Carey and Jason had been married for a week.

"Run, Jason. Just run away. Hide in the mountains," Carey begged.

"They would find me. It would be worse than joining up, and we would still be apart."

Then Carey put into words what Jason could not.

"We cannot survive without each other. If you go, you must come back. Can you do that?"

HOME

Jason looked into her eyes and said, "Your grandmother said our destinies will be entwined forever. I believed her then and I believe her now, so I will do what you ask."

CHAPTER TWO

Jason

Jason avoided the war meetings like the one in Pruntytown; instead, he went directly to a recruiting office. The patriotism of the war gatherings had gotten to the point of lunacy. Veterans would spout off about fighting and the heroism of it. Patriotic maiden women would wave handkerchiefs and flags and talk about joining up except for the fact that they were women. Some towns filled their quotas in less than an hour; one young man after another would sign to prove their bravery. These soldiers were usually sent at once to a camp and many were killed or wounded before they had been in the field a week.

After signing the documents, Jason stood hat in hand in front of the commander of his newly formed regiment and asked, "Sir, I am requesting a furlough."

Without looking up from his desk, Major Oley said, "You've been here two days and you wanta go home?"

"Yes, sir!

"Why?"

"Carey asked me to come home and help her prepare for winter. The word around camp is we aren't moving out for at least a month. So I thought . . ."

Major Oley looked up at the boy in front of him and answered, "Good enough. Be back here in ten days. If I have to send someone, you will be shot."

"Yes, sir. I plan on fighting, but Carey comes first."

As he left the tent, he felt the major's eyes on his back. He knew he did not understand, but Jason didn't care; each step took him closer to Carey. The ten days was more time than he expected. He walked back to his quarters, gathered his belongings, and started for home.

From over his shoulder, he heard a soldier yell, "Where're you headed, hillbilly?"

Jason turned in the direction of the shout, and walking backward along the path, he yelled back, "Home to my mountains and my woman. The Johnny Rebs will have to wait to die for ten more days." He turned and walked on amid catcalls and henpecked jokes, none of which fazed him. The war could wait; Carey needed him.

CHAPTER THREE

Carey and Jason

Jason had been gone for a week; Carey knew it would take him three days to walk to the closest recruiting office. She had no idea whether he would be granted the furlough or how soon. Her grandfather who fought in the War of 1812 said that if he joined a new regiment, he would get the leave, but the duration of it might not be more than a couple of days. Carey prayed that Jason would get enough time to make it home for a few days. Even two days would give them time to prepare the farm for winter and time left over to start a family. Carey had made up her mind that by Jason's next furlough, if the war lasted that long, he would come home to a son.

Every fifteen minutes or so, she would walk out onto the porch and look up the hill to the "waiting spot," knowing that he would be sitting there. After interrupting her work over and over she realized nothing would get done at this rate. She headed out to the barn to feed the animals, vowing that she would not check for Jason until all the animals were bedded down.

After five days, she had settled into a daily rhythm. She was actually starting to enjoy the solitude during the day, but at night, Jason's absence would be unbearable. She stayed up late, mending by lamplight because she knew when she laid her head on their pillow, she needed to be able to fall asleep from fatigue, or she would lie awake until morning, sobbing. She thought, *This war can't last long. I cannot bear it.*

HOME

On the morning of the sixth day, she walked onto the porch threw out the bathwater, and glancing at the waiting spot, saw movement. She leaped off the porch and ran toward the creek; it was Jason. They met in the creek bottom, the same way they had most every day since their youth. Jason kissed Carey gently, and they walked hand in hand to the cabin.

"You look mighty weary," Carey said.

"Well, it's a three-day walk, and I made it back in two," Jason exclaimed. "We have a lot to accomplish in six days."

"Six days? I thought you'd have ten."

"You're forgettin' the walkin' time. So let's not waste time talking."

"Where do we begin?"

"Right here," Jason chuckled as he pushed Carey backward onto their bed.

*****

Carey slipped quietly out of bed, leaving Jason asleep, and went outside to do her morning chores that had been interrupted by Jason's arrival. She fed the animals and gathered eggs, grabbed an armful of firewood, and cooked some breakfast. Jason watched her from the bed, almost forgetting about the troubles that were brewing elsewhere.

He had not come through town on his way home for fear someone would ask about the war. He had only been in the army for a few days, but he knew a Union soldier might not be welcome in this area. There was not a clear line about which side the western Virginians would take, but he was a mountain boy, and his guts told him the South was dividing the country. He didn't think one man owning another man was right. A man should get paid for the sweat off his back, so he chose to fight for saving the United States of America.

Carey interrupted his political thoughts.

"Hey! You gonna lie in that bed all day? We got a farm to prepare for winter."

"As soon as I finish my breakfast, woman," Jason said playfully and hopped up. They went right to work side by side.

The day was approaching when Jason's furlough would be over. Carey rushed through her morning chores and was putting breakfast on the table when Jason came in from the barn.

"Well, we have done it," he said as he hung up his coat on the hook beside the door of the cabin. "Everything is in order. You and the animals should have plenty of food for winter, and I'll be home for spring planting."

"That sounds great." Carey tried to sound excited, but in fact, she was really feeling depressed. She feared this would be their last meal together for a very long time. Jason had packed the night before and laid out his uniform. She had spent most of the night sewing on the buttons and some trim. He would look sharp, but her concern was for how long. *Please, Lord, no bullet holes to repair in the spring,* she thought.

Jason had walked up behind Carey and, putting his arms around her, said, "You'll be fine until I get back. I know you are strong enough to handle just about anything."

"Just about is right," Carey responded, "anything but you not coming back."

"I will promise that barring any unforeseens, I will be back in the spring."

"Yeah, well, it's the unforeseens that worry me."

They sat down across from each other and ate their meal without any talk of the war, and when they had finished, Jason gathered his kit and walked onto the porch. Jason looked around the small mountain property, trying to embed all the details in his brain. He wanted to be able to close his eyes and imagine this place where Carey would be waiting, the next few months.

Carey joined him on the porch, and while they stood in silence, the connection between them was obvious to them both. Jason turned toward Carey and said, "I love you. I will see you soon." He said it matter-of-factly like he was leaving for a day's hunting.

Carey understood what he was doing and replied, "I love you too. Have a great hunt. Come home safe."

HOME

They embraced briefly, and he started across the field toward the creek and the path up the mountain that was hidden under the sycamores. Carey stood on the porch, waiting for him to appear at the waiting spot. He waved as he passed, and she waved back; she was glad that the tears on her cheeks were not visible from there. When he was gone, she went inside to clear the dishes and tidied up just as she would have if he was coming home for dinner.

CHAPTER FOUR

Jason

After he had waved at Carey, Jason turned up the mountain and quickened his pace. He would have to push hard to make it in to camp before roll call. It wouldn't do to be late; Major Oley was not joking about shooting deserters. As Jason hastened along the mountain trails, he couldn't help but notice how beautiful the woods looked with all the leaves turning. He did not look forward to descending into the Kanawha Valley. Charleston was an exciting place to be at the beginning of this war, but he hoped he didn't have to stay in the city for long.

The best part of being in Charleston was the mail; it was delivered regularly, unlike some of the other outposts. Carey's letters poured in, bundles of three or four at a time. From late fall until March, the Eighth Regiment saw little action; her letters were a welcome relief from the boredom. When orders came for their march to Little Creek to join General Fremont's Mountain Department, Jason hastily wrote Carey a note because this movement meant his spring leave was canceled.

It was April, the spring of 1862; Jason had not imagined that the war would have lasted this long when he joined up. It would soon be a year since his departure, but he had managed to keep the memory of the life he would return to foremost in his mind. Carey's letters gave him assurances that she was fine and learning to do everything the farm and the home demanded. He had known she could survive without him; she had always been fiercely independent. Occasionally, he would worry that she just might not need him when he returned.

During the year, Jason had seen some action as his regiment pursued Stonewall Jackson up the Shenandoah Valley. He had followed Carey's instruction, keeping his head down, and so far had avoided any wounds. He could not say as much for his comrades. Shortly after joining up, he had met a fellow West Virginian who had chosen to join the North as well. His name was Samuel. They had become immediate friends because of their love for the mountains where they had grown up. Much like Jason, Samuel had a wife at home, struggling on the family farm. They had many conversations about returning, not as heroes but just alive.

On this particular day, the regiment was chasing General Ashby, Jackson's rear guard. Everyone knew General Ashby by reputation. Jason was able to see the prancing black stallion from his position on the hill. Even from some distance, Jason could understand why the man was always described as striking. He sat his horse tall, and Jason's best description would have been *knightly*.

Samuel hollered from a nearby post, "Jason, shoot that bastard's horse and be the hero of the day!"

Jason lowered his rifle and took aim. He had not been given an order except for Samuel's. He turned back to answer Samuel and watched the bullet hit. Samuel fell dead instantly. In anger Jason raised his rifle and fired; General Ashby's horse toppled to the ground. Jason's satisfaction at his retaliation was short-lived when Ashby drew his pistol and called, "Charge!" Jason climbed down to Samuel's body and bowed his head, thinking of their homes. Samuel was nineteen years old. General Ashby, the "Knight of the Confederacy," also died that day, but Jason would mourn only his friend.

CHAPTER FIVE

Carey

In the bright, dewy morning, she could push her worries out of her mind and go to work. The days turned into weeks and the weeks into months, and in quick order, the months were shaping into a year. Carey had settled into living alone and taking care of everything the little homestead required. Her daily routine involved all that she had been doing before Jason went off to war and all of what he had been doing as well. Her workday was usually sixteen hours of well-organized chores, leaving her very little time to ponder on her loneliness. The last thing she would do when she fell into bed, exhausted, was to pray that Jason was safe and on his way home to her.

The first thing each morning, she would pray for his safety and write a paragraph in her weekly letter. She never knew if he was receiving the mail, but she kept him up on all the happenings at home—well, not all the news, which would have had to include her monthly visit to town to check the casualty postings. Carey never looked forward to her trips to town; besides the two-mile trip, her mother and father would always try to talk her into moving in with them. She knew they thought Jason was already dead or lost, but she would convince them he would come back to her. Her insides continued to tell her he was coming back, and Grandmother always backed her up.

"Carey, you know, Jason and you are connected. You will know if anything happens to him. Keep praying and search your heart for him. Be steady. Go home."

Her parents would frown at them and shake their heads, but they would not contradict Grandmother. So the argument would be over, and she would start her trek back to the mountain sanctuary she and Jason called home. She would ride the mule into town and walk on the way back while he carried the month's supplies. When she first started making the trip to town alone, she worried that some home guard or deserters would hide in the woods to rob her, but after ten months, it wasn't so frightening. In fact, she had never actually seen anyone on the trail. She had gotten in the habit of approaching the cabin from different directions, always stopping at the lookout points to make sure everything looked undisturbed before winding her way down to the clearing.

Stopping at the lookouts always brought back vivid memories of Jason. Carey would look across at the opposing lookout, hoping he would be sitting there, looking back at her. Some days, if the light was just right, her heart would leap in her chest, and she would blink her eyes and watch the image fade. It was just wishful thinking, and it always made her cry, which in turn made her mad for being weak. Wiping the tears away, she would use the visions to strengthen her belief that Jason was standing on a battlefield somewhere, thinking of her.

In her next letter to Jason, she would tell him to think of her often so she would be able to visualize him sitting on the hill, looking down at their cabin, because even though it brought tears, it always strengthened her. How many more months would she need to endure? In his last letter to her, Jason had talked about camp life and how the talk was that the war would end soon.

Carey wrote back of her disappointment about them not starting a family before he had left, but she knew she could not have stayed on the farm alone if she had been pregnant. It had been two years since they had said their goodbyes. The last letter she received from Charleston came months after it was written. His unit kept taking him farther away from her. Sometimes she wished he had joined the Confederacy; they weren't marched north for training and rest. Jason would talk of the boys he had met from Illinois and Michigan; she didn't even know where those states were. She and Jason had told no one that he was fighting for the Union cause. Even though the mountain folk were trying not to take sides, she was living behind enemy lines. Most of the town where her family and her grandmother lived were Confederates. The Home Guard were lenient as long as no one caused trouble. Some of the townsfolk would discuss the war from both points of view, but unless there were actual young fighting men in town, the discussions never escalated into argument.

By the summer of 1863, some of the young men had returned maimed, and most of the small community had suffered the loss of at least one son. The women and children were so overwhelmed with staying alive and feeding themselves, they no longer cared about what went on off the mountain. The old men still talked of war, but the talk was of their own harsh experiences, not of the present plight that their sons and grandsons were dealing with. It was incomprehensible that the casualty list contained fallen Union and Confederate from the same family.

Carey had managed to stay out of town for months by asking her family to check the casualty list. She had no reason to go in for supplies because there were none. She still had the mule, a milk cow, and a few chickens. She was especially glad that Jason had taught her to shoot when she was fourteen; squirrel hunting had kept food on the table. Every time she sat down to a meal, she prayed that Jason was eating, and thanked the good Lord for not fulfilling her wish about starting a family. It was enough to feed herself. Whatever would have been her plight if she had been pregnant three years earlier?

CHAPTER SIX

Jason

Jason continued to write letters to Carey even though he knew that she would most likely never receive them. The Eighth marched to Little Rock and joined up with Fremont's unit. The Mountain Unit trained snipers. Jason had proven himself a marksman early on when he took down a horse from three hundred yards during a skirmish. His officers chose him to join an elite group of soldiers who would have special assignments. Jason was not sure what this meant, but he did not hesitate. He had been promised some furlough, so he started imagining going home to the mountains for a few days.

Instead he found himself marching away from his beloved mountains north for training in Pennsylvania and finally Ohio. Each step he took tormented him as the distance between Carey and him increased. His new assignment took him into country he had never seen. He started to have a fear that he would not be able to find his way back. The only good thing was there was less actual combat the farther North they marched.

After several weeks, they made camp in the Ohio valley near Chagrin Falls.

It was beautiful rolling country with plenty of local game, and they ate meat for the first time in many days. Jason tried to describe his experiences in a letter to Carey.

Just as he signed it and folded it to mail, Nathaniel approached him and said, "Do you know what we are going to be trained to do?"

Before Jason could answer, Nathaniel blurted, "Assassins! We are going to climb up in trees and shoot Rebels like deer when they walk by on their way to wherever."

"Where'd you hear such a thing?"

"In the mess tent, overheard some officers talking about it. They figure we can pick off an entire patrol before they get off a shot as accurate as we can be."

Jason thought that over for a minute and said, "Yeah, ten of us in the right trees could pick off twenty of them before they knew what hit 'em."

"Well, I suppose you're right, but ain't that just plan outright killing?"

"It's definitely an ambush, but fighting like Indians in a war like we got might be really helpful. If the patrols are stopped, the enemy won't have any way of knowing where we will attack from or where we are for that matter. It's just good strategy. When do we start?"

"Sounded like real soon. I guess that's fine with me. I'm tired of sitting around, thinking about home."

"That's a fact. Let's end this war any way we can."

CHAPTER SEVEN

The Rape

Carey and Jason's cabin was not on a main trail, and only the local mountain people knew its whereabouts, so anytime Carey saw someone pass by, she paid them no mind. Folks who knew her might give a holler from the mountainside and come in for a spell, but it happened very rarely. The war had curtailed any friendly gestures for someone living so remotely. It was lonely, but she did feel safe.

One night, just about dark, she noticed a group of two, maybe three, men pass by the opening in the trees behind the cabin—the place where she used to watch for Jason's arrival when they were kids. They could have been hunters headed back to town; she hoped they had had some luck and, with their game bags full, would be headed home to their families. It did surprise her that they didn't walk like old men or boys, but as she sat rocking on the porch, the significance of her observation did not hit her as important. Shortly after the sighting, she folded up her sewing and moved inside to replenish her fire and prepare for bed.

Suddenly, the door of the cabin burst open, and a filthy-looking man with a beard dressed in Confederate gray stood leering at her. She glanced at the shotgun over the fireplace, but he got to it first. He stared at her while he slowly cracked the barrel and, finding it loaded, snapped it shut and pointed it at her.

"What have you got to eat?" he shouted.

As Carey backed away, she tried to think how this situation should be handled. She looked the man squarely in the eye and, trying to keep the quiver out of her voice, said, "Put the gun down, and I will warm up some beans for you."

He seemed to relax a bit, but he did not lower the gun.

"Why should I trust you. Ain't your man fightin' for the North?"

"My man's been gone a long time. I don't know whether he's fighting or not."

"You go on and warm them beans, and we'll decide about the gun later."

Carey busied herself at the fire, turning her back on the intruder, hoping he would consider it a gesture of compliance. She swung the heavy iron pot back over the heat and stirred the beans slowly. The man sat behind her at the dinner table that Jason had built with his own hands. She began to formulate a plan of action, but maybe this man was just hungry and, after he filled his belly, would be on his way. Who was she kidding this was wishful thinking?

She heard the chair scrape the floor as the man got up. She watched him walk slowly to the sideboard and pull down Jason's jug. The moonshine had been sitting in plain sight. With the shotgun in one hand and the jug in the other, he pulled the cork with his teeth and took a long draw. Then he stared at her again, and what she saw in his eyes made her shiver. She tried to appear self-assured as she ladled the beans onto the tin plate. She didn't want to get close enough that he could touch her, so she slid the plate down the length of the table. He stopped it with the gun, still watching her with his cruel eyes.

"You stand over there where I can see ya, ya hear."

Carey didn't answer; the place where he indicated was near the door that hung loosely from its hinges because of his violent entry. At least it was a chance, but where would she run to? Maybe she could hide along the creek bed and slip off to town later. Carey waited until the man had started eating his meal and bolted for the door. She ran toward the outhouse, knowing she could dodge around it into the thicket and work her way to the creek. Just as she reached the outhouse, the door swung open, and a second man grabbed her by the waist and threw her down on the ground. Carey fought back, but he was bigger than the shifty-eyed man she had escaped, and after he had brutally raped her, he threw her over his shoulder and carried her back into the cabin.

He tossed her on the bed and exclaimed to the other man, "You didn't wait for me for dinner, so I didn't wait for you for desert."

Carey watched as they ate the beans, finished off the shine, and packed most of what she had left in the house. It appeared as if they were leaving. Then, the shotgun was lowered into her face by the big man, and his partner had his way with her as well.

"No fair. You took all the fight out of her," he commented as he buttoned his trousers, and then they were gone as quickly as they had arrived.

Carey lay on the bed, feeling dirty. She must have cried herself to sleep because when she awoke, the light of the morning sun was finding its way into the cabin. When she tried to get up, her body wouldn't cooperate; it was screaming in pain. She was bruised and turning awful shades of blue and purple. Her first thought was to go to her parents and tell them how stupid she had been to stay in the woods alone, but how could she tell them what had been done to her? No, she was strong; she would just go on like nothing had happened. No one would know; she could live with this secret and the shame.

She pushed herself out of the bed, took the bedclothes to the washpot, and with determination, pushed them into the water to soak. She balled up the quilt that she had made for her bridal bed that was torn and bloodstained and threw it in the fire. As she watched it burn, she made a vow that she would tell no one, not even Jason. It would be the first secret she had ever had that he would not hear.

For the next few days, she watched the trails closely. She prepared her cabin for a second attack; this time she would not be caught off guard. The next person who came to her door unannounced would regret it. The dogs that she had kept in the barn would be chained at the front door, especially Jason's big catch dog, Yankee.

She kept her hunting trips closer to the cabin and left areas of the trail in and out brushed clear of tracks so she would know if anyone had come or gone when she returned. She would sit at the "waiting spots" for at least a half hour, watching the cabin before returning. Whenever she sat in Jason's place, she would cry; she hoped he would feel her fear and come home to her.

In her weekly letters to Jason, not knowing if he was receiving them, she talked of his eminent homecoming. He had been gone for close to three years. If he still loved her, it was time to come home. Her grandmother had told her not to lose hope; she would know in her heart that he was coming back. He had promised.

As the weeks passed since the incident, Carey became obsessed with being safe. She hung noise makers in the trees surrounding the house even though at night the sounds frightened her. The dogs would create a ruckus in the middle of the night, and she would bolt upright with the loaded shotgun aimed at the door—the door that now had a strong oak plank reinforcing it.

When eight weeks had passed, she made the walk to Grandmother's house; she had been feeling poorly and, with no explanation, went to her for advice. Grandmother was sitting on the porch, dozing, when she walked up. Carey was glad that her parents would be in town; they always went to check the casualty lists on Tuesdays. It frightened her to see her grandmother snoozing on the porch so unprotected.

When her foot made the steps creak, Grandmother said, "Good afternoon, child. What has brought you to me?"

"I haven't been feeling like myself. Thought you might have a remedy for what ails me."

"What kind of ailment?"

"I don't rightly know, but most of the morning, I just don't feel right."

"Come close and let me look at you." When Grandmother took her eyes away, there was worry in them. Before Carey could ask what was wrong with her and what flowers or roots she would need to find for the remedy, Grandmother said, "When was Jason home? Why didn't he come by to see me?"

Carey looked at her with surprise.

"Why would you say such a thing? You know I haven't heard or seen my Jason in three years."

"Oh, Carey, dear, come put your head in my lap and explain to me what has happened to you. My dear child, you are pregnant."

Carey's eyes filled with tears, and she fell on the porch floor, grabbing at her grandmother's knees. Her grandmother soothed her as best she could, and Carey told her what had happened.

When she had finished, her grandmother said, "Tell no one. Return to your cabin, and I will send you help."

"But, Grand, how will I survive, and what will I tell Jason when he returns?"

"We will have to wait and see about that, but if this is what the good Lord has given you, it must be handled carefully."

She reached behind her rocker and handed Carey a small bag and said, "This will help with the morning pains. Don't lose hope. Help will come."

CHAPTER EIGHT

Daniel Sawyer

Daniel returned to the mountains to find his mother dead and his father missing. Some said his father walked into the mountains the day after his younger son, John, was listed as dead, and no one had seen Jacob Sawyer since. Daniel had been wounded. His head injury and the loss of his right arm had prevented him from writing, and the family had presumed him dead. He went to Carey's grandmother for some guidance. She told him to go visit with Carey and tell her she had sent him to help.

Daniel was reluctant to go to Carey and Jason's cabin. The last time he had seen Carey, she had been angry with him for trying to talk Jason into going to the recruiting rally. He had watched his friend Bailey die and, out of fear, had joined the wrong side that night. Even though that night was a really long time ago, it seemed like only a minute or two.

He was glad that Jason had stayed with Carey because if he hadn't, he surely would have died before joining the Rebels like he had done. When talk of the war had started around home, it was going to be over quickly. Daniel figured which side really wasn't going to make a difference; either way, you had to fight. Jason said the Union was the right side; saving the country at any cost was his belief. Besides, the western Virginia boys had no need for slaves. Their mountain farming was best done by kinfolk who understood the climate and the mountain growing seasons, not by black fellows with no mountain sense.

Jason said, "When the time comes, I will fight for the Union." Daniel wondered if he had fought opposite him anywhere over the past three years. What if he had killed him? He had heard of brothers finding brothers on the battlefield. If losing an arm had gotten him out of this war, he was glad for it.

He had spent his first night in the army hunkered down inside a covered bridge in a heavy rainstorm. The commanding officers assumed the Yankees would be hold up somewhere out of the rain too, but they were wrong. When Colonel Dumont's artillery opened up on the town, Daniel was aroused instantly. All the recruits in the covered bridge heard orders from every direction, and there was utter confusion. Colonel Porterfield was hastily putting together a plan, but leaving this bunch of raw recruits to defend the bridge was poor judgment. When the Yankees under Colonel Kelley advanced, Daniel was on his feet, running to the south; he wasn't sure if he had waited for the signal to retreat or not. When they regrouped in the town of Beverly, he heard there were twenty-six assumed dead. The first skirmish of his soldiering career was over, and he had not proved himself worthy of any uniform blue or gray.

Since that day, he was determined he would not act cowardly again, and he guessed he had done all right. Daniel perceived that the idea of soldiers having an "eagerness for the fray" was absolutely not true. Some men he met said their first encounters may have been that way; that was not true in Daniel's experience, but afterward, being warm and having food in their stomachs had become much more important. The officers knew what lay ahead, but the soldiers stumbled into battle more often than not.

When he woke up in the hospital with his head bandaged and pain in his right arm, his relief to not be in a Yankee prison somewhere up north made him weep.

The nurse who was attending him, thinking his distress was over his arm, leaned in and offering him some water, said, "They will send you home to your family soon."

Daniel looked up at her and said, "As soon as my head clears, I'll be sent right back to my unit."

"No, son," the doctor who had just walked up said. "Amputees go home."

"Amputees?"

"Your right arm, soldier."

Daniel raised his right arm painfully and tried to wriggle his fingers, but his eyes told him the truth of it. The fighting had been difficult, but not fighting would be a totally new challenge. He thought about his dead comrades and remembered someone saying, "Soldiers are but human, and the men who have been in battle before know what is implied in the work ahead, and some will not answer at the next roll call." Daniel looked up at the doctor and said, "When can I start home?"

Daniel was determined that he could deal with this new battle as well as he had learned how to be a soldier. He had been shot over and bloodied; he could make himself comfortable. He had learned to cook and to take the weather as it came and say no more about it. So he would march home to his family and be a one-armed mountain farmer.

When he found he had no family and no home, Yankees had confiscated all Confederate holdings in the township. Grandmother's advice was to go help Carey. He wasn't sure how much help he could be, but he set off immediately for Jason and Carey's cabin. He hoped he would remember the way.

CHAPTER NINE

Carey

Carey left the cabin before daylight to do some hunting to replenish her food stocks. She hoped today's hunt would yield a deer, a small buck, or a big doe. She needed to put up enough meat to carry her through until spring. Several weeks had passed since her visit with grandmother, and she knew that with each passing day, she was nearing a time that hunting and walking too far from the cabin would not be feasible.

She followed the creek about a half a mile and settled herself in a thicket not too far from an obvious watering hole. She hoped she wouldn't have to wait too long in the damp grass. After about twenty minutes, a doe with a late fawn appeared. Carey hesitated when she saw that the fawn was too young to take care of itself. The doe caught her scent and darted away; Carey was relieved.

As the sun rose higher in the sky, another doe entered the clearing and suspiciously crept toward the water; she kept glancing over her shoulder but not in Carey's directions. Carey leveled her gun at a place where the trees opened up behind the doe and waited. When the buck appeared, Carey waited for him to turn toward the drinking doe and this time, without hesitation, took her shot. It was a kill shot!

Carey leaped to her feet as the doe disappeared in to the thicket with a crash. She was almost positive the buck was dead, but she drew her knife so, when she reached him, she could cut the jugular to expedite the death. He was about 160 pounds, enough meat to feed her for the rest of the winter. Her first thought was she could share the backstrap with Jason in the spring when he returned. Her next thought was much more practical. When the bleeding slowed, Carey positioned the deer on its side and, starting at the base of the jaw, made a long cut to the tail. She pulled out the guts and all the unusable parts. This process was of course made worse by her condition; thankfully, her morning sickness was subsiding each day. She forced herself to concentrate on the task at hand. After deboning and organizing all the meat, she wrapped the skin around it and positioned it on the travois. The carefully wrapped bundle sat evenly balanced, and now that the weight was reduced by about 70 pounds, Carey had no problem dragging it down the hill toward home. Her chances of going hungry were eliminated; 80 to 90 pounds of meat properly stored would mean no more need for hunting until after the baby arrived.

Carey had learned early on that transporting the game to the cabin was always easier if she hunted uphill. She had brought the travois with her on her back like she had seen the Indian women do. She had fashioned the harness herself. When she got close enough to the cabin, she could whistle for Yankee, and he would drag it across the creek bed and up the short rise to the barn.

Carey started her trek back to the cabin and, as was her habit, stopped at the lookout. There was a man crouched on her front porch. Her heart began pounding; could it be Jason? Whoever he was, the dogs were crowded around him, tails wagging furiously. As she studied on him, he turned and looked up toward the spot where she stood. Carey ducked down and tried to slow her breathing.

Then she heard the shout.

"Carey, is that you? It's me, Daniel."

She recognized his voice, so she stood up in the opening and shouted back, "Daniel, oh my god, I'm coming down," and she whistled for Yankee. Yankee didn't take long to get to her since he could just cross the creek and come straight up the side of the mountain. She rearranged the travois, harnessed the dog, and continued down the winding trail that led to the cabin.

When the dog left his side, Daniel started up the trail from the opposite direction and met Carey coming down. He gave Carey the best one-armed hug he could muster and exclaimed surprise at her buck. She found herself rambling on about all the things she had learned to do since Jason left, mostly because she didn't know what to say about his condition. Daniel was about a hundred pounds lighter than when he had left, and he was the first man she had known with a missing arm. She had seen other boys around town with similar injuries but no one she had known before. Daniel watched in amazement as Carey stored the meat and supplies from the buck with efficiency; she had a use for every part.

Carey hadn't had very much company at the cabin since the day Jason left after his furlough, at least not wanted company, she thought, and quickly stopped the memory of that evil day from rising to the front of her mind. Turning to Daniel and without thought, she blurted out, "So how'd you lose your arm?"

The expression on Daniel's face was startling, but she couldn't take back her words. Obviously, his war-related experiences were every bit as brutal as hers, and losing an arm could not be compared to gaining a child, even a child sired by a despicable deserter.

Realizing that Carey had not thought before speaking so bluntly, Daniel stopped to think before saying, "Well, I do miss it, and washing one hand should be easier, but without the other un, it can be tricky. As to how I lost it, I got no clue. When I came to, it was gone along with some other things."

Carey didn't know whether to laugh or cry, so she said, "Let's fry up some of this deer and celebrate your homecomin'!"

After supper, Carey tried to steer the conversation away from the war and asked Daniel about his plans.

"Carey, I am here because Grandmother sent me. She said you needed my help, but now that I'm here, I don't see why. Your place looks in great shape for winter, and there is enough meat ready to store. What possible good can a one-armed man be to a woman as capable as you?"

This time Carey thought before opening her mouth; apparently, Grandmother did not tell Daniel the whole truth. Jason had been gone so long. Carey didn't want to think he was dead, but there had been no word for months. This baby would need a father. Was this Grandmother's plan? Daniel could not be called back to fight, and most people wouldn't notice the discrepancy in dates. He could complete the family, no one need know about her shame, and the baby would not be branded a bastard; even Daniel wouldn't know any different.

"I do need your help, Daniel. I'm so lonely. Please stay and keep me company."

"Carey, what about Jason? I know how much you care for each other, and besides, I can't be a real husband. I didn't just lose my arm."

Carey dropped her head onto the table and began to sob. Daniel clumsily put his arm around her shoulders and said, "What do you need me to do?"

Without lifting her head, Carey said, "Oh, Daniel, I'm pregnant."

"But how? You said Jason hadn't been here in more than three years. Is he hiding in the woods, a deserter, what?"

Again, without lifting her face, Carey told Daniel the secret she had sworn never to divulge with all the details. She was astonished at how easily it spilled out and, once told, how much better she felt. Daniel felt bewildered, but once again, he stopped himself from saying anything. Grandmother had known about his condition just as she had known about Carey's. They could pull this off without being untrue to Jason, because like Carey, Daniel loved Jason; he was his best friend and like a brother.

Placing his hand gently under Carey's tearstained face, he lifted her head until their eyes met and said, "I will protect your secret with my life. No one knows when I came back to these parts, and only Grandmother can dispute it, and we both know she would go to her grave before she would tell anyone."

CHAPTER TEN

Jason and Ethan

Nathan's hope that they would be leaving Pennsylvania and headed back into the fray was not to be the case. There would be many more days of the camp boredom before deployment. Jason was more than happy for the delay; he wasn't ready to face the sheer terror of battle. He actually began to think that shooting the enemy from the cover of trees would be less terrifying; he was continually justifying the strategy of it to others in his company.

They were all issued either a Sharps rifle or a Whitworth, but some of them already owned custom-made target weapons, known as "sporting" arms. Instead of endless hours of drilling, Jason and his companions would practice climbing trees with their rifles, which could weigh as much as thirty pounds, figuring the most comfortable position they could find and still shoot accurately.

After two days of practice, Jason realized his sight was off. His accuracy was definitely not what it had been; something was wrong. He fired another round and knew for sure, he had a problem. He would have to hunt down a blacksmith or a gunsmith to rectify this issue.

He shouted to the officer in charge, "Permission to come down?"

"What's wrong, soldier?"

"Got a problem with my scope and maybe more, not sure."

"Yeah, I noticed you were off your game, not sure you hit anything you was aimin' at, kid. Come on down."

Jason swung the rifle onto his back and clambered down from his perch. The officer said, "There's a guy who works in the officer's mess that can help you."

Jason looked at Captain Black and said, "The officer's mess?"

"He was a gunsmith before he joined up. The other boys say he is a wizard with rifle modifications. Those two fellows with the custom jobs knew him before the war broke out. Don't waste any time. I need you back in that tree."

"Yes, sir, on my way," Jason exclaimed. "I like it up in those trees. I'm ready to kill Johnny Rebs."

Jason left his rifle tied across his back and started through the camp to find this blacksmith and gunsmith turned cook. As he walked, his thoughts drifted to Carey; he thought about what he would say to her the next time he saw her. He wondered if she was okay and how badly the trials of the war had affected their hollow. He knew the cabin he had built could withstand any inclement weather, and its remoteness would be an advantage against most marauders. There was really no reason to be on the trail above the cabin except to know it. He guessed someone could stumble onto the creek just as they had all those years ago, but all in all, she was probably as safe there as anywhere else. He justified safer, but something told him he was wrong.

He said a silent prayer, "Please, God, keep her safe from harm."

Jason walked on, suddenly realizing that the camp that he was a part of was a lot bigger than he had previously believed. His company prepared their own meals and lived apart from the others—partly by design and partly because the nature of their training was different and not too well thought of by some of the enlisted. He had been so lost in his thoughts, he hadn't noticed the stares or the comments that drifted his way until now. He became aware quickly when a dirt clod smashed into his boot. He looked around quickly at the group of soldiers gathered by an old caisson.

They stared back at him and one shouted, "Don't shoot me, sniper," with dripping sarcasm. Jason wanted to respond but knew he was outnumbered, and fighting would only get him a night on guard duty or worse. He simply walked on. Why could they not understand that his job was going to make them safer? Then he noticed how young they were, raw recruits; they had not seen it yet. After one skirmish, they would understand—at least if they survived. Jason raised his head, shifted his rifle, and trudged on toward the mess tent.

Jason knew he couldn't just walk in the front door of the officer's mess, so he skirted around the tent to the back. He rounded the corner, almost falling over an older man in a ragged uniform, peeling potatoes.

"Ah, sorry didn't see you there," he exclaimed.

In return a low growl emanated from the slumped body.

"What do ya want?"

"I was sent here to find the gunsmith?"

Without looking up, the figure said, "You're one of those murderous sharpshooters."

"Now hold on," Jason shouted.

The man lifted his head. Jason saw nothing but pain in the man's face. As he unfolded his body to its full height, Jason realized even his anger at being called murderous would not help him. He started to think of how to finish his statement without provoking this man.

Jason softened his voice and slowly said, "I just do what I'm told, and if it saves lives on our side, I guess it's the best I can do."

Jason flinched as the big man extended his hand and said, "I'm the gunsmith you're looking for. My name's Ethan Henderson."

Jason stepped forward, shook the man's hand, and with a cautious tone, said, "Name's Jason and I need your help."

In a low, sad tone, Ethan said, "You have no idea how much help you will need. Show me the problem."

By this point, Jason wasn't sure what they were actually talking about, but he lowered the rifle from his shoulder and handed it over. Ethan took it and walked slowly across the enclosure to a small tent. He threw open the flaps, laid the rifle on a wooden table inside, and proceeded to disassemble the gun.

Jason looked around the area with interest. It was a complete gunsmith shop; there were vises and a variety of tools, obviously well cared for and purposefully used. Ethan was concentrating on his work and Jason was afraid to interrupt, so he watched quietly. After about twenty minutes, Ethan looked up surprised, then he asked, "Where'd you get this rifle? It's definitely not standard issue. This was special made!"

"It was my daddy's. A friend of his modified it for him." Then Jason added, "He was a gunsmith too, the friend, not Dad."

"Where do you hail from? You're not from this area are you?"

"No, sir, I'm a West Virginia boy. They marched me up here to train because I'm good with that rifle."

"I bet you are, and you're in luck 'cause I know this rifle, so I can fix it, maybe even make it better."

"What do you mean you know it?"

"Come over here and I'll show you," Ethan said. "Look right here." He was indicating a place on the inside of the gun plate, which he had removed. Jason held the plate to the light, and etched in it were three letters, JEH. "Those are my Uncle Joe's marks. He must have been your daddy's good friend."

Jason could see old Joe's face bent over the guns in his shop, and the memory of all those days he spent there fell over him like leaves in the forest. He learned to shoot right outside of that shop. His father and Joe corrected his stance and told him how each rifle's balance would affect his accuracy.

Ethan interrupted his thoughts.

"Return to your unit. Come back in three days, and your rifle will be ready."

"How will I train for the next three days without a rifle?"

"You tell your captain, Ethan says you don't need more training."

Jason wanted to protest, but Ethan had returned to his inspection of the rifle. Jason quickly decided he would rather be thrown in the guardhouse than confront this man again—the same man he had almost punched less than an hour ago; when he looked at Ethan, he knew he should just go. Ethan was deep in thought, but his memories had creased his brow, and the sad pain from earlier had returned.

Jason hurried away, walking briskly through the camp once again, ignoring anyone who called out. He arrived back just as his platoon was gathering for drilling and his fellow snipers were climbing trees. As he approached, Captain Black looked up and scowled. Jason formulated how to respond to the question he knew was coming.

"Where's the damn rifle, soldier?"

"Left it with the gunsmith, sir."

"How do you expect to perform your duties without a rifle?"

Jason thought before speaking; after all, this was his commanding officer.

"The gunsmith said it might take a couple of days to finish the repair."

"Do you expect me to believe you let a complete stranger take your custom-built rifle? Wasn't it your father's before you?"

Jason suddenly felt sick to his stomach; had he given his rifle away? He was such a fool; it could have all been a pack of lies. Not wanting to admit his stupidity, he turned to Captain Black and said, "Ethan said I didn't need to practice with any other rifle."

"You spoke personally with Ethan?" he said.

"Well, yes, he is the gunsmith you sent me to."

"I sent you to the gunsmith tent, but Ethan works in the mess. How does he know you?"

"Apparently, my dad knows his uncle Joe back in West Virginia, but if he recognized me personally, he didn't let on."

"Okay, you have a three-day leave. I don't want to see you again until you have your rifle in hand."

Jason was so thoroughly confused, he found himself speechless. Captain Black shook his head and walked away. He had so many questions, he didn't know where to start. He walked to behind the firing area and sat down on a stump at the cook fire to ponder on his morning.

CHAPTER ELEVEN

Jason and Ethan

Three days later, Jason retraced his steps and found his way back to the gunsmith. He found Ethan in his shop, working on his gun.

He looked up and said, "Good timing, I'm just finishing up."

Ethan's broad shoulders hid the workbench from Jason's view. He came forward, and looking around the man, he saw a gun that was very similar to his own. It had a tiger maple wooden stock from butt to muzzle and a forty-one-inch barrel. Jason studied the distinctive grain a moment, realizing that it was his rifle, but all the silver and brass inlays had been removed. His first thought was that this strange old man had stolen from him, but the silver and brass still lay on the worktable in plain sight.

He cleared his throat and asked, "Is that how I pay for the repair?' indicating the silver pieces.

Ethan laughed.

"No, take it with you, after this is over, you can have it all put back, even the fancy inset patch box."

Jason's confused expression made Ethan laugh again and add, "I suppose you thought the Rebs wouldn't be shooting back. The trick is to be hidden from view. A plain gun does not reflect the sun. The hidden man lives longer. You must try to find hate for those men called the enemy. Do not forget, across the way, the same thought with the same end, death,"

"Ethan, you talk like a man who knows a lot about this bloody business."

"I have experience with the killing of men from a distance. It started as revenge and ended in service for the Union. It leaves a scar on your morality that is hard to shake. You be careful, Jason. Don't let the sharpshooter's psychology turn you into something less than human."

Ethan put the silver and brass pieces in a small leather pouch and hung them around Jason's neck. He gave Jason a final handshake, handed him the rifle, walked him to the tent opening, pushed him out, and dropped the tent flap in his face. Jason stood numbly, holding the rifle, wondering about what had just transpired. After several minutes, he turned and headed back to his unit. Perhaps Captain Black could offer some sort of explanation.

Jason and Nathan

Jason hurried through the encampment, but there would be no time for explanations; his unit was preparing to move out. Nathan met him in the road with his meager belongings and shouted, "At last we go to kill the Johnny Rebs!"

Captain Black led his sniper unit out of camp at a quick march for a distance. After about a mile, the unit turned right, and the road narrowed into little more than a trail rising steeply. Captain Black slowed the speed and pointed out some rock ledges to the left. They scrambled up the side of the mountain, individually looking for a perch. Jason went forward with Captain Black since he was considered the best marksmen he would have the privilege of initiating the fray.

Jason realized immediately that this location had been scouted, and the ledge he and the captain were approaching had been prepared. It reminded him of the lookouts that he and Carey had above their home. He pushed that thought away; what he was preparing for should not be connected to his old life in any way.

Captain Black said, "Find a comfortable location, and your targets will pass through at the fork in the road below. You will have to wait for the second unit. No one will fire until you do. Do you understand?"

"Yes, sir, but who is the first target?"

"This man is planning to demolish everything in his path. You do not need to know who he is. Understood?"

"Yes, sir," Jason replied. Even if he was given a name, it probably wouldn't have meant anything to him. He thought about what Ethan had said and tried to build some hatred. If his was the first shot, would there be return fire? This appeared to be an ambush. The enemy would be taken by surprise; they were fighting like Indians. His inner voice said, *You will follow your orders. Killing the enemy will stop the enemy from killing you and yours.*

He settled into his position and surveyed the target area below. Resting the rifle on a rock ledge, Jason sat facing downward toward the trail. Captain Black had managed to get them into position quickly and safely before full daylight. It was not unlike hunting the deer on his mountain at home. If you could get in place just ahead of daybreak, the quarry was relaxed and unprepared for invasion. The birds were tweeting merrily, and a complaining squirrel was chirping arrogantly. The first sounds of the patrol were the clanking of swords and soft hoof beats of walking horses picking their way along the road. The soldiers were singing quietly the strains of "Lorena," a favorite among both armies. Jason once again began thinking of Carey and home. Jason pulled his mind back to the present and took aim at the rock he had chosen that would put his shot at chest high on a rider. The first horse's head appeared in his sights. He watched it pass through and counted the column through. He took a deep breath and slowly exhaled then, a second, let out about half of it. Jason saw the officer's epaulet and touched the trigger. The heavy rifle cracked. The projectile reached its mark before the sound. The patrol was in a complete panic when the other members of Jason's unit started firing. Jason sat in shock and watched the slaughter unable to reload.

Captain Black ordered, "Reload. Take out another target, soldier!"

Jason did as he was ordered and began firing. He had perfected his reloads to about every ten seconds. After his third shot, he did not reload. The captain touched his shoulder and said, "Reload. What are you waiting for?"

Jason saw the look in Captain Black's eyes but still refused to load then he said, "Don't waste any more shot. They have retreated."

Jason looked down at the road below. There were bodies covering the road, horses milling about riderless, and total confusion in the retreating soldiers left with no officers to answer their inquiries. Jason looked up at his commanding officer and said, "What have we done?"

"We have done our job. It's what you trained for all these months. Mission accomplished," Captain Black responded without emotion.

Jason didn't feel like anything had been accomplished. When the unit joined up, the others were all talking about the kills, the mission. Jason sought out his friend Nathan. He found him sitting alone in their tent. He looked up at Jason with a look of pain.

"My cousin Jake was killed today. He was among those soldiers on the road."

Jason didn't know what to say, but he thought of the pain in Ethan's eyes and began to understand. When he and Nathan, from the mountains of West Virginia, had joined the Union forces, this was not a scenario they considered. Today they had shot and killed their kin. Nathan asked to be returned to a regular unit and was killed a few weeks later. Jason thought about doing the same but realized he was more likely to make it home again if he stayed a "hidden man," a sniper. Several missions later, he surrendered himself to the work and began to kill mechanically and without remorse. He pushed for individual assignments and was soon considered the best assassin available.

Jason stopped writing to Carey; he just didn't have anything he could share with her. The killing was pushing him further and further away from any connection with normal folks. He had isolated himself from the other soldiers after he learned of Nathan's death. He still thought of Carey and wished that he could go home, but the war dragged on, and there was always someone the officers wanted dead. He followed his orders as precisely as he aimed and began to consciously think of the targets as nothing more than targets. He remembered Ethan's comments all those months ago when he had repaired his rifle, and now he understood the sadness in Ethan's eyes.

Ethan had been a one-man sniper unit after his entire family was murdered and his home was burned to the ground. His killings were motivated by revenge in the beginning. He was asked to continue his service as a sniper when the war broke out, and for a while, he continued to shoot assigned targets. Then while riding back to camp following a mission, he was confronted by a boy, who was maybe fourteen years old, carrying a small child in his arms. The child sagged limply in his arms; she had been shot.

Ethan stopped his horse and asked the boy, "How did this happen?"

The boy replied, "From out of nowhere, sir. She was dead before I heard the shot."

Ethan knew she had been caught by a sniper shot that missed its target. He himself was too accurate, but a missed shot could travel for miles. The soldier who fired it would have only reloaded and fired again, never knowing the consequences of the missed shot. He rode back to camp and asked for a reassignment. He never picked up his rifle again but was ordered to work as a gunsmith. He felt it was a penance. In this way, he could make the guns more accurate. He justified his past life with the hope that he might save lives during the rest of the war. When Jason heard this story, he was in too far to find a way back to normalcy, so he had soldiered on. He was overwhelmed with sadness most of the time. He could only pray that this insanity would end soon.

Jason had scouted this spot for almost two weeks. He had found an appropriate location that allowed for an open view of the ferry crossing below. He had cleared just enough of the branches to have a clear shot, but to even a keen observer, his presence would never be suspected. The distance to the target would be well over three hundred yards. Jason had already discerned the downhill trajectory and chosen a back target. He had been living in a nearby cave for almost a week. Black said it would be easier if he wasn't seen going and coming from the camp. Jason had found the solitude refreshing, but sitting on the side of the mountain reminded him of Carey. His dreams that were normally nightmarish became restful and comforting. His waking hours brought back the darkness of his soul and the fear that Carey was lost to him forever.

The spies had reported that his target would be coming across the river on the next morning. Jason made his final preparations with the last rays of the setting sun, prepared a meal of the rabbit he had snared, and fell asleep to the sounds of the mountain. He awoke a little before dawn, climbed down to his perch, and awaited the arrival of the old man that operated the ferry. The old man followed a routine that Jason had watched each morning, but today, before he had fully prepared, a lone rider appeared on the opposite bank.

The man, his target, shouted, "I'm in a hurry! Move it along!"

Jason had to stifle a laugh when the old man looked up and went right back to his slow movements without a word. He thought, *If I were you, I wouldn't be in such a hurry to die.*

The ferry began to move slowly across the river. The "target" did not even dismount; he rode his horse onto the ferry and remained mounted. Jason quickly recalculated for the higher target. He decided it would be easier on the old man's nerves and arms if he took the shot closer to his side of the river.

He rested his rifle on the branch he had chosen earlier and took careful aim. He locked in on the third shining brass button on the uniform, took a deep breath, exhaled, took that second breath, exhaled about half of it, and pulled the trigger. The gun cracked loud in his ears; the "target" toppled onto the deck. The old man stared in amazement at the dead man, then he heard the crack of the rifle and hit the deck.

Jason gathered everything he had brought to the ledge and walked back to the cave. It would be several hours before the shooting would be reported, so he sat down to read an old letter that Carey had sent. It had taken almost a year to find him. He looked at her neat handwriting and felt his heart jump; he still loved her so. He turned the letter over in his hand and, for the first time, noticed the date scrawled across the back, July 14, 1863. He had joined the Union cause on July 14, 1861 that meant that his three-year enlistment would be ending soon. The Pennsylvania unit he had been assigned to had actually been slowly moving closer to Harpers Ferry, which meant home was about a three-day walk from their present camp near Moorefield. Carey could help him climb out of this hole; maybe he could go home. Jason quickly broke down his cave camp and actually felt excited about talking to Captain Black and getting started on the mustering-out process.

For the first time in a year's time, Jason felt hope; he had served his country, the Union was winning, and the war was ending. Three years was a long time to be away from his precious Carey and the mountains of his youth. As he walked through the main camp, he ignored the stares of the regular soldiers; in his rush to return, he had not discarded his sniper gear. He laughed out loud at the thought of his appearance. Unlike three years ago, these were veterans; they did not make disparaging remarks at the sharpshooter. In fact, if they knew his reputation, they were afraid. He was a murderous man and to be feared.

Jason went straight to Captain Black's tent. He stood at attention until his salute was returned.

"Stand at ease, soldier. Mission accomplished?"

"Yes, sir! Mission successful and completed," Jason responded.

"Good work, Jason!"

When Jason did not leave, Captain Black looked up.

"Is there something else to report?'

"Yes, sir. My enlistment is up next month, and I was hoping to start the mustering-out process."

Captain Black swung away from his desk to look at Jason.

"Are you seriously thinking the Union Army is going to let one of their most valuable assets go home at this time?"

Jason tried to hide his disappointment. He slowly formed a plan in his head, looked his commanding officer in the eye, and calmly said, "I will be leaving."

Black noted the look on Jason's face and answered, "Get some rest. We'll talk tomorrow. Dismissed!"

Jason spun on his heel and walked out.

CHAPTER TWELVE

Daniel and Carey

Several months had passed since Daniel had moved in with Carey. The first two weeks had been awkward; they moved around each other, careful not to bring up either the losses that Daniel had suffered or Carey's expanding belly. They fell into a routine of shared chores. Daniel slept in front of the fire, so around five thirty every morning, he arose, dressed, and headed outside to the outhouse and returned with an armful of firewood. Carey rolled out of bed as soon as she heard him close the door, dressed quickly, and rekindled the fire. Before Daniel came back in the house, she headed to the well for enough water for the day, set the water on the porch, gathered the eggs, and made sure all the livestock were where they were the night before. Hopefully, fence repair would not be part of today's work; it meant working side by side, and Carey was becoming more emotional each day. She figured it was just her condition, but she really didn't want to raise the child without some assurances.

Daniel was glad to have a place to stay, and helping Carey was so easy; she had spent so much time alone, she had everything worked out. The day was always routine. His morning jobs included bringing in firewood, feeding the dogs, bringing in stock, or turning out stock. Except for the hogs, all these chores were perfectly workable for a one-armed man. He knew Carey had consciously thought this all out without including him in her decision. He watched her belly grow and wondered if he would be included when that time came.

He very much wanted to be a part of this misfit family, which was a direct result of this horrible war that made very little sense to the mountain folk.

When the marauders left, they took Carey's mule, leaving her no way to plow a field for planting. Daniel did the best he could with one arm, but even with both of them working, the outlook was bleak. They needed to prepare at least an acre for a barter crop, enough to feed the two of them and the rest to trade for all their other needs. Carey's belly had started to protrude, and Daniel grew more worried about what he could do.

"Carey, we need to face facts," Daniel started slowly. "We need to give up and move in with Grandmother before it is too late."

Carey looked at him with all her independence and determination clearly displayed on her face and said, "You do whatever you want. I will not leave my home. When Jason comes home, this is where he will find me, dead or alive."

Daniel felt the sting of Carey's voice, and the mention of Jason reminded him that the feelings he felt for her would never be returned. Jason was his best friend, and he knew how much he loved Carey. If he were alive, he would have come home by now; the war was, after all, winding down. He tried to think how to answer. Before he could respond, he noticed a movement on the hillside and heard a loud crash. Carey had already started running in the direction of the commotion. Daniel followed at a run. He caught up to Carey at the creek.

Lying in the creek bed was a horse completely entangled in harness, attached to the trace that must have ripped free of a caisson. He had a fist-sized hole in his neck that went through to the other side. Daniel stood paralyzed at the sight. Carey had pulled her hunting knife and was carefully cutting away the useless harness.

"Daniel, don't just stand there. I need help."

"What exactly do you think you are doing? It has an infected hole in its neck. Obviously, he has been shot."

"We are going to save him, and then he is going to save us. Don't you see? He will pull the plow!"

Daniel realized it was a long shot, but Carey was right; it could work. He jumped down into the creek bed and began to assist Carey. She looked at him with a kindness that made his heart leap.

The task ahead of them was not going to be easy. The musket hole was the worst of his injuries, but the poor beast had multiple wounds covering 80 percent of his body. Luckily, he was so exhausted from falling down the side of the mountain, he didn't struggle or kick out while Daniel and Carey cut away the remaining pieces of leather. Carey grabbed the remnants of the reins and pulled; the horse struggled to his feet. He was knee-deep in the cool creek water and seemed content to rest there.

Carey stroked his face and said, "You're going to be okay, my good boy."

She turned to Daniel and said, "Go to the house and get some clean cloth and soap. We can use the creek water to cleanse his wounds."

Daniel hurried to the cabin and found the things Carey had requested. When he got back to the spot where the horse was standing, Carey had already started cleaning the blood off his front legs, chest, and shoulders.

Daniel looked at the poor creature for the first time. He was covered with blood and mud from ears to tail. He was standing with no weight on his right hind leg, which had a ragged tear about two inches below his hock. Daniel stopped himself from voicing the doubts that crept into his head.

Carey looked up at him and said, "Let's call him Aslan because he will need the heart of a lion to pull through this."

Daniel climbed down into the water and prayed, *Please let this go well.* Without a word, he gently began to clean out the wound in the right hind. Surprisingly, "Aslan" stood quietly throughout, listening to Carey's soothing voice. It took almost forty-five minutes to complete the cleaning; they stood back and looked at their bright bay horse with two white socks and a blaze with a bloody cavity in his neck.

"Let's take him to the barn before starting on the hole," Carey announced deliberately.

"Let's take a bit of time to think about how to treat the wound. We are going to need some of Granny's herbs," Daniel said.

"You're right, but I got everything we will need at the cabin. Granny taught me how to tend to a gunshot wound after Jason left for war. I'm glad to use it on a horse instead of my man."

Carey walked Aslan along the creek to a place that wasn't too steep for him to clamber out with his three good legs. He somehow managed to launch himself out but then needed to stand and rest awhile before continuing the climb to the barn. It was slow and arduous for all three of them. Daniel tried to help Aslan keep his balance by holding his tail, and Carey encouraged him from the front. He hobbled along; his right hind was causing him a great deal of pain. Daniel hoped he would recover enough to pull a plow and make all this effort worthwhile.

Eventually the trio made it to the barn. Once inside, Carey stroked the horse's neck while Daniel filled a bucket with well water and found a little hay to throw down for him. If they could avoid looking at the gaping hole and the resting hind limb, he could have been any working horse in the county. Arm in arm, Daniel and Carey headed into the cabin to prepare for the next veterinary session with Aslan.

Daniel sat down at the table and watched as Carey pulled out boxes of herbs from her storage area. She glanced in his direction and said, "Fetch me a double handful of acorns. We need to make a poultice." Daniel did as he was told, ignoring the double handful reference; he knew she didn't say it with any malice of forethought. It wouldn't have occurred to her that he was still affected by the loss of the arm. Once a soldier was removed from the fray, the regular folks just assumed it all stopped. Daniel supposed it did for some soldiers, but his body reminded him daily of what he had lost. He gathered the acorns and returned to the cabin. Carey had water boiling when he came in, and he dropped the acorns in with a pluck.

Carey had the mortar and pestle on the long wooden table, and she was slicing up a piece of the hard rootstock of several bulrushes. She dropped each piece in the smooth bowl and slowly ground it to powder using the pestle.

"While I do this, crush those bunchberries up. We can put them on the deeper wounds or anything that may have been a burn. It will sooth him and stop the burning and maybe some of the itching as well."

"Are those chicory leaves? We should boil them down for a poultice for his right hind leg," Daniel interjected. Carey looked at him with that same look of surprise Daniel had grown accustomed to; it seemed she had never taken him too seriously. Of course, she never really knew him before; he was Jason's friend. Daniel guessed she had never been impressed with him, and he hadn't really given her any reason to be. Most times he and Jason were together, there was always too much drinking and cavorting.

Carey was astonished that Daniel knew what a chicory leaf looked like, much less its uses.

"That's a great idea," she finally said. After a few minutes, Carey asked, "What else do you know about medicinal plants?"

"What I know I learned from Grandmother before I left. And then, in the hospital, there was a woman who worked with all the amputees." Daniel faded into silence.

Carey hoped she would have the courage and the fortitude to hear all of Daniel's story when he was ready to tell her. She sensed that this was not the time. They needed to concentrate on Aslan's physical recovery; he could help them survive the winter.

Carey stood up with a sigh, gathered the sides of the cloth with the bulrush poultice in a small bundle, placed it in a woven basket along with the jar of crushed berries and Daniel's still-warm cloth inundated with boiled-down chicory leaves and flowers, and headed for the barn. Daniel followed, noting Carey's expression; healers believe that the power can be felt in the love of the patient and the faith in the Creator. The preparation and dosage of the herbs they were using were derived as much from Carey's heart as from her knowledge. Carey looked over her shoulder and slowed her step until Daniel was at her side and said, "We do this together. The power to heal comes from the plant, the Creator, and our love."

Daniel quickly let all the negative thoughts fade away, and as he placed his hand on her shoulder, they entered the barn. Aslan lifted his head slowly from the hay he was eating and backed away as Carey entered with the basket. He seemed to know he had more to endure. The lower edge of the wound on the left side of his neck was draining. The entry wound, now that it was clean, didn't look too bad. Carey gently applied a thick poultice covering the entire area. She studied on the draining side and decided the bottom should remain open. Carey cupped a handful of the bulrush poultice and pressed it onto the upper portion of the wound, leaving a small area where it was already draining open. She had prepared it well, and it adhered well.

While Daniel wrapped the right hind leg, Carey stood at Aslan's head and steadied him. He wasn't completely receptive to having the wrap applied and knocked Daniel off his feet. As he sprawled on the floor, Daniel wasn't feeling the love so much. Carey was amazed at how Daniel wrapped and secured the horse's leg with just the one arm. She almost laughed when he used his head for balance but knew it would have been insensitive. Her earlier comment came back to her; she knew it hadn't gone unnoticed. She really needed to be more careful.

Together they doctored all the little cuts and scrapes with the bunchberry and stood back to survey their work. The red blotches caused by the bunchberries and the brownish-green poultice made him look like a carousel horse. Carey and Daniel turned toward each other and began to laugh. Aslan went back to his hay with a look of indignation.

In the weeks that followed, Aslan healed quickly; the bad wound in the right hind closed over nicely and left only a small bump and surprisingly no limp. Daniel was amazed at the healing, but Carey had believed all along that Aslan would be ready for plowing when the time to plant had come. The hole in his neck drained for many weeks, but the poultice and Carey's careful cleaning prevented an infection.

Luckily, the harness collar did not sit anywhere near the wound. So when it was time to plow, Aslan was ready and willing. The work seemed to suit him. Carey believed he must have worked a farm before the war. Aslan had come home. Perhaps it was an omen; she hoped it was a good one.

CHAPTER THIRTEEN

Daniel and Carey

Daniel had been formulating how to initiate a conversation with Carey concerning their future. They needed to think long term. Right now all they could do was get through each day, and in the process, he thought they were getting further apart. It was time to ask her to marry him so the child would enter the world without any stigma. He needed to talk with Grandmother. He finished up with the livestock, harnessed the horse in preparation for work, and planned a trip to town.

As he headed to the cabin, he heard Carey talking to Yankee.

"What can I do, boy? I will have to let him go if this child growing inside me is going to be okay." Carey had not seen Daniel approaching when he suddenly appeared at the corner of the porch. She drew back in alarm at the expression on his face. He looked angry.

"Why would you let me go?" he snapped.

Startled she said, "You misunderstood!"

He turned to Yankee and said, "Maybe you can explain. She chooses to discuss things with you."

Carey looked at the dog then at Daniel and, unable to contain herself, burst into laughter.

Daniel could not figure out her behavior as hard as he tried; he spun on his heel angrily and headed back to the barn. He was going to visit Grandmother.

As soon as Carey got control of herself, she rushed down the incline to the barn. She arrived in time to stop Daniel from climbing onto Aslan's back.

"Where are you going?"

"Away from you. The longer I'm here, the harder it will be to go."

"But I don't want you to go. I need you! The baby needs you. I was talking about letting Jason go. He's most likely dead." When she finished her speech, her face was wet with tears. She looked up at Daniel, waiting for his reply, fearful he would not believe her.

Daniel had such mixed emotions; in that moment, he realized admitting that Jason could be dead was the one thing neither of them wanted, and Carey had said it first. She was the strongest woman he had ever met or known. He understood why Jason had chosen her.

He placed his hand on her shoulder and lowered himself to one knee.

"Carey, can you marry me? I want to be the baby's father."

Carey pulled him up to her, and for the first time since Jason left, she felt safe as Daniel closed her in his one very strong arm. When the moment passed, they stepped back and Daniel said, "How do we go forward from here?"

"Together," Carey quietly replied.

They walked to the house hand in hand. Daniel knew that in spite of her outburst, he would never take Jason's place in her heart, but being needed was enough for this damaged man. Everything would be for the unborn child. Because of his war wounds, he could not father a child of his own blood, but now he could have a family.

"Tomorrow, we will visit grandmother and ask her blessing on our family," Carey said.

Daniel nodded his reply. After breakfast, they returned to the day's chores. Daniel started to clear the top field, and Carey prepared a midday meal. When the cabin was in order, Carey pulled out her sewing and continued working on the shirt that she had been making for Daniel to replace the rags he had come home with from war. She smiled softly at the shortened left sleeve and how strong his arm had felt.

After sewing on the last button, she folded the shirt she had made and placed it in the trunk with her wedding gown, closing the lid. She decided no one would object if she wore the dress again. It would need some alterations, she thought with a shudder, but nothing would hide their obvious secret. Thanks to Grandmother and this terrible war, all the real secrets could be hidden forever.

Daniel followed behind the poor old horse dragging the plow through the rough ground and thought about Jason. He wondered how he had met his end and if he would approve of what he was doing to help Carey. He only hoped that he would forgive him for falling in love with her. She was, after all, an amazing woman. Knowing how this child had been conceived only made him admire her more for talking of its future in a caring matter. They would make a good end of all this.

CHAPTER FOURTEEN

Carey, Daniel, and Jason

Carey stepped onto the porch and tossed the dishwater onto the grass. The pups scrambled out from under the house, and momma dog lifted her head. Carey leaned down to give her a haphazard pat. The baby shifted inside her and slowed her raise. At that very moment, Jason was looking through his gunsight at his beloved wife. Carey felt a strange sensation and quickly glanced in the direction of the lookout; she had not kept them cleared after the marauder attack, and the trees and rhododendron had quickly filled the spaces. She stopped herself from thinking there was someone there. Today was the beginning of her new life; she would need to let Jason go for good.

Jason lowered his gun and fell back into the leaves. When he looked through his scope a second time, he had realized that the man was Daniel. He closed his eyes and let himself go back to the good memories of his youth and this cove. He could not find one childhood memory that did not involve Carey or Daniel. The woman whom he fell in love with at ten years old was now living with his best friend. The anger began to build inside; he would make them his last mission. After all, this was a Confederate soldier living with his wife. He was trespassing on a decorated Union soldier's land. Jason sat up found the fork of a small tree to rest his gun. He decided to shoot the woman first; the one-armed man would not be able to react quick enough to arm himself before he was dead. Jason took a deep breath and then another; letting the second breath out halfway, he closed his finger on the trigger.

Carey put her hand in the small of her back and stretched as far as her protruding stomach would allow. At that moment, Jason thought of Ethan and the little dead girl on the road and dropped his hand from the trigger. Lowering the rifle, he knew he must still have a thread of the man he was; he could not kill an innocent unborn child. He would leave Carey and Daniel in peace. He gathered his belongings and started back up the trail the way he had come. There was no reason to stay. He had lost everything he cared about in the three years of fighting, including his own self-respect.

Jason had been missing from his command for more than a week. It had been an arduous journey through the war-torn mountains to arrive back at the cove. He had heard of men who had rejoined their units without execution; perhaps his heroic killing would still make him an asset. If luck was with him, he may have never been missed; he had quartered apart from the unit, and he had avoided any friendships after Nathan was killed. However, he was sure when he didn't check in with Captain Black, he had most likely sent someone to check on him. If he was shot for desertion, he would never see Carey or Daniel again. He resigned himself to whatever fate awaited and trudged on.

His trek back to Moorefield proved less intense than the trip to Summersville. He knew which trails were frequented by Home Guards and where the homes were friendly to the northern cause. The small groups of men he had met on the trail were mostly just mountain folks like him heading home; some were most definitely deserters, but when he didn't question them, they passed by without comment. Jason stayed vigilante and cautious with all that he met, but at the top of the ridges, there were fewer travelers, and he made good time.

The second night, he found an abandoned cabin and prepared to spend the night under a roof. Just as he started to douse the fire, he heard a horse approaching. He stepped back from the light of the fire and cocked his pistol at his side.

The rider dismounted and hollered, "Coming in!"

Jason shouted back, "State your business."

"You're trespassing," the voice said.

"Looked deserted to me," Jason responded.

"That's 'cause I been fighting Mr. Lincoln's War," came the response.

"Are you mountain born?" Jason asked.

"You bet I am, and if you ain't fightin' at the moment, neither am I. Can I come in?"

"Yes, but come slowly and show me your hands."

As the rider entered the light, Jason took a deep breath and holstered his pistol. He knew this man; he had seen him through his gun scope. It was the old man from the ferryboat. He did not relax entirely, but he didn't really think the old man was a threat; he walked with the weariness of a long ride and arthritic bones. He grabbed a stump from the wood pile and flopped down on it as close to the fire as was safe. Jason threw another log on, raising the level of light to where they could study on each other awhile.

After a few minutes, Jason said, "You look mighty old to be serving in any man's war."

The old man looked up at Jason took a moment to gather his thoughts and began to tell his story. "My name is Jonathan Thompson. I grew up down the back side of this very mountain. This cabin and the summer pasture around here has been in my family since before I was born. It was my great-grandpappy's first homestead. So trespassing you are, as far as I know, you're the first person who has stumbled across it in these three years. When my wife died and my older boys left for the fightin', I went to join up. Like you say, I was too old for real soldiering, so they give me a spying job. They put me in business as a ferryboat operator so's I could inform about anyone going and coming.

"So I ran the ferry and I watched people. I also watched for a particular person because part of my payment for the spying would be the death or arrest of one man. If I gathered enough evidence, I was told that this particular Home Guard captain could be taken out. You see my home and family were destroyed because we were northern sympathizers."

He watched Jason closely. He had spoken without knowing which side this boy had been fighting for; that could be a mistake.

Jason said, "Relax. I'm not fighting for anyone at the moment, but what I've done was for the North."

"Are you an outlier or a deserter?"

"Neither, you finish your story and maybe I'll tell you mine."

"Fair enough," and the old man continued. "That man came onto my farm while I was up here huntin'. He threatened my wife and tried to take my younger boys off to war. Said they'd been drafted even though we already had two boys off fighting. When Momma refused, he cracked her skull with his pistol, and then when my boys went after him, he shot them both and set fire to the house. They was just younguns, barely old enough to carry a full pail of water. I saw the smoke before I reached the road. Their mother lay there half-conscious and watched her sons bleed to death. Her last words to me were 'You put that man in a grave.'

"My family dead and buried, I abandoned the ruins of my home and started working on a plan to track him down and do just what my sweet Ellie asked with her last breath. It was like destiny when that Yankee officer put me on that ferry. The worst part was I had to see the murderer of my family every week or so, and he always had another tale about northern sympathizers that he had eliminated.

"I listened to his tales and slowly put together enough information, which I then relayed to the right people. My cousin would bring me lunch each day, and he could then report to the Union camp about the things I heard and saw. I reported to the Rebels too so I wasn't suspected of being biased. I had to make sure they didn't shoot me for being a spy."

Jason was beginning to understand where this tale was headed, and he was debating as to whether he should admit who he was to this poor old man who had been through a bad time. The old man tossed another log on the fire. He was just about to ask Jason what his story was when the light of the fire revealed the rifle behind Jason, leaning against a tree. His words hung in his throat, and Jason followed the old man's gaze.

Instead of coming right out with the question that the gun raised, the old man looked at Jason and began again.

"About a week ago, I was able to put that man in a grave. Not by my own hand, of course, but dead either way. He was shot by a sharpshooter working for the Union army. Shot at my request, payment for services rendered. That shot came from over three hundred yards. When I heard the sound, that menacing, evil man was already dead. Did you know there's a guy over in Tennessee been making shots like that for the Confederates? They say he has a gun kinda like that gun yonder."

Jason then realized this old man was thinking about this wrongly. With assurance he said, "I was not sent here to eliminate a spy. I stumbled in here by mistake. Didn't know you were coming. In fact, the only reason I didn't shoot you was 'cause I recognized you from a week ago."

Then, all the tension faded away from the old man's face, and he started laughing. You know, belly laughing like he had just heard the best joke ever. Jason started to laugh as well. All the worries about losing Carey, even his concerns about being a possible deserter, fell away. The old man reached in his sack; Jason's hand dropped onto his sidearm until he saw the jug appear. The old man held the jug out to Jason and said, "Best shine in nine counties. Let's drink to life!"

The two of them spent the rest of the evening talking about their mountain homes, the beauty of the forest, and speculating on where this crazy life would take them from this point. The old man reminded Jason that looking forward was the only way to wash the past away. He also told him that someday, when the anger subsided, he might come home and hear from Carey the complete story after all the war had affected everyone. Their meeting was not atypical of the stories he had heard while operating the ferry; many paths crossed in this conflict, some in good ways, some in tragic ways.

CHAPTER FIFTEEN

Jason, Jim, and Johnny

Jason and the old man had a companionable and leisurely breakfast before saying their goodbyes. The old man planned to stay and told Jason he would always be welcome at his fire. Jason thanked him for his advice and began the trek back to his unit, still hopeful that he would not be shot. He decided it would be best to arrive after dark, so he spent the last afternoon at the sniper nest above the ferry crossing. He was surprised to find the cave undisturbed from his last stay. A family of field mice had moved in, but no signs of any human visitors. He found it odd that Captain Black had not sent someone looking in the one place he knew he had been before his request to be released. Jason counted the days since he had said he was leaving in the captain's tent. Technically, he had been gone a full week without permission. When he didn't show up the next day, Captain Black probably ignored it. The next day, he may have sent someone to his camp area, but those fellows would have covered for him. They couldn't have said where he was because he never said anything to most of them. Jason thought it most likely took four days before his absence was even questioned. The thought did occur to him that he hadn't been missed at all. The nature of his assignments kept him out of sight regularly.

A couple of more hours and he would sneak into camp and, with a little bit of luck, start heading away from his past like the old man had suggested. He lay back on his nature-made bed and dozed off. Jason was awakened by a movement at the cave's entrance, then he heard voices.

"Do ya think we're in the right place?" said the first voice.

"I hope so. I've done enough climbing for one day. Who is it we're looking for?"

"That sniper, Captain Black has a job for him."

Jason had quietly picked up his pistol and, aiming it at the entrance of the cave, said, "You fellas better show me your hands or you're dead!"

The two young soldiers walked into the entrance with their hands over their heads in obvious fear. The look on their faces almost made Jason laugh, but he tried to maintain his menacing demeanor. He lowered his pistol and said, "Come on in and sit."

The two soldiers, not much more than boys, warily entered the small cave and sat cross-legged on the ground. Looking around, the taller boy said, "This is kinda comfy. You been here long?"

It struck Jason funny that they were acting like visitors in his home.

"Not too long. Where you boys coming from?"

"Well, Captain Black sent us to find you two days ago, but we got lost on the way. We're from St. Louis, and we're not very good in the woods."

Jason chuckled a little and responded, "I knew from your accent you weren't mountain boys. Did the captain send orders, or do I have to check in with him?"

Eyeing the two rabbits Jason had snared earlier, the other boy said, "Are you going to eat those?"

Jason smiled at his luck and said, "You know, boys, I think we'll have those for dinner and report in tomorrow. What do ya think?"

"That would be the best thing that has happened to us for the last two days."

They moved outside the cave to build a cook fire, and as the rabbits cooked, Jason learned more about Missouri and the Midwest than he thought possible in a very short period. Johnny and James were city born and raised. Their description of St. Louis sounded like lies to Jason, but these two kids were incapable of such. Jason knew that their very nature would make their story ring true, and his fears of being shot for desertion were gone, for as far as anyone would know, he had never left his cave.

The following morning, James and Johnny escorted Jason into the main camp; he promised not to tell Captain Black they needed his assistance to find their way back. The two boys entered the officer's tent first, and Jason waited outside. In short order, they were dismissed with not a little bit of shouting and name-calling. Jason pulled back the flap and saluted Captain Black. He returned his salute and, without any mention of the other day's discussion, handed Jason his next assignment. It was an ambush, the type of assignment that Jason had gotten away from, but he knew from the expression on the captain's face it was indeed a punishment for his insolence. He left the tent, praying it would be the last ambush he would be involved in and thanking his fate that he would not be placed in front of a firing squad.

CHAPTER SIXTEEN

Daniel and Carey

Daniel had found and restored an old two-wheel cart. He had been waiting for the appropriate time to unveil it. He had awakened earlier than usual and harnessed Aslan to the newly painted cart. He tied him near the front porch in preparation for the trip to Grandma's. Carey had gotten to the point in her pregnancy that she had to let Daniel do more of the chores on his own. Carey could hear Daniel whistling as he went about the morning chores, and it made her smile to realize how much more adept he had become in everything it took to run the farm. He had learned to accept his handicap during the last few months, and he had to be the strongest one-armed man she would ever know. She imagined there were a lot of one-armed men meeting this challenge all over the country and was glad that she was able to help one good man get on with his life. Today was the beginning of the rest of her life as well, and thanks to Daniel, she had a direction to go.

Carey climbed out of bed, washed her face, tied her hair back with a piece of blue ribbon she had been saving for this day, and packed a basket with brunch for the ride into town. She wasn't looking forward to the ride. She was heavy enough that sitting astride Aslan was not comfortable, and she also felt guilty that Daniel had to walk. She looked around the cabin, thinking, *After today, this will be Daniel and Carey's cabin not, Carey and Jason's cabin.* She tried to tell herself Jason would have been okay with all of this, but it still didn't feel right. Grandmother had told her she would know if Jason were dead, and if that were a fact, then Jason was still alive. However, even feeling that way, Carey knew her course was set. Today Daniel would become the father of the child, and this innocent deserved to enter the world with a safe environment.

Daniel waited on the porch for Carey to emerge; he wanted to see her expression when she saw the cart. He was well rewarded; the smile that crept over her was illuminating.

"Oh my, when, how did you do this?" she exclaimed, "It's amazing!"

Aslan stood tall and proud as if he also knew today was a special day. His harness was adorned with bright fall leaves, and the cart was edged with pine boughs. Daniel had commandeered the porch-swing cushion for the seat. Carey could not imagine how Daniel had kept this hidden from her, much less done all the intricate work. She extended her hand, and Daniel helped her up into the cart. She was so pleased to think that he did it all for her.

"I don't know what to say," Carey uttered as Daniel climbed in beside her.

"You have already said it. Today we start our family. This is my wedding gift to you."

The trip to town following the creek road was quiet and pleasant. Carey tried to keep a light banter going but found herself falling into long silences. Daniel was apparently lost in his own thoughts because he didn't seem to notice her mood change. It had become their custom to stop in a small glen near the creek for brunch. When the cart stopped rocking, Carey looked up, startled they had arrived so quickly. Daniel helped her down and went to get water for the horse. Carey sat alone for a moment. Without telling Daniel, she walked off to the right of the clearing; working her way through the underbrush, she found herself at the tree—the tree where she and Jason had carved their names all those years earlier. Because of the war, their initials were still just as they were that day. Jason had never returned to the tree to add the letter to her name as he had intended.

Forever is truly a long time, Carey thought.

"Carey? Where are you?" she heard Daniel yelling. There was worry in his tone.

"I'm here," she called. "Nature called."

They had a companionable snack and finished the ride to the little white chapel that was within walking distance of Grandmother's cabin.

Daniel proudly parked Aslan and his festive cart at the church doorstep. The preacher was waiting at the altar. If he noticed Carey's condition, he made no sign of it. He nodded in Grandmother's direction as she sat in the first pew and began the ceremony. It bothered Carey that the church was so empty; she had expected some well-wishers. She knew the little town was full of loss and mourning, but even a wedding as odd as hers should be a celebration. Grandmother stood and thanked the preacher.

Grandmother turned. When she reached the double doors, she said, "Come on, you two!" with an obvious twinkle in her eyes.

Daniel kissed Carey on the cheek, grabbed her hand, and half ran to the back of the church. She started to resist and then knew her future was beginning. The small lawn outside the church was crowded with the townspeople, and fiddlers began to play as Daniel and Carey appeared on the steps.

Grandmother turned to the gathering crowd and said, "I now present to you Mr. and Mrs. Daniel Sawyer, here today to announce the pending birth of their first child."

A cheer arose from all who were gathered, and as Carey and Daniel descended the steps, Carey began to cry.

Daniel said, "Are you all right?"

Carey turned to him and said, "Of course, and thank you for making this work." And stroking her belly, she could only think of the future; she would let the past go.

Two weeks later, Carey delivered a healthy baby girl, and she named her Catherine Emerson Sawyer. Daniel had agreed that using Jason's last name, Emerson, was not inappropriate under the circumstances. The townspeople thought it was a great memorial to Jason even though the child was Daniel's. No one knew the truth except Grandmother.

CHAPTER SEVENTEEN

Jason, Jim, and Johnny

Jason returned from his "punishment" ambush with even more depression. It was another slaughter similar to how his sniper career had started, the one that had taken Nathan from him. He had lost Carey, his best friend Daniel, and his only wartime comrades, Nathan and Samuel, all because of this terrible war; he wasn't sure how to go on. Fortunately, the weather turned cold; snow fell overnight, stopping almost all camp activity.

Jason entered Captain Black's tent and simply stated, "I'm going to the cave. Send Jim or Johnny when you need me again." Jason knew he was tempting the officer's rage, but he didn't care. Even a deserter's death would be better than this pain. He turned and left, fully expecting a minié ball in the back, but it never came. The further he got from the encampment, the lighter his burden felt. At the cave, the solitude brought sleep; he was so weary.

Fortunately, Captain Black had no assignments for Jason at this time, so he passed the time preparing his quarters for winter. About five miles away, the soldiers in the encampment were also preparing for winter. The stand of trees that had provided shade throughout the spring and summer wouldn't provide much protection when the snows came. Jim and Johnny were shaping a lean-to with whatever they could scrounge.

"You know, that sniper is as snug as a bug in his cave," Jim said to Johnny.

"That guy is a little scary, but you're right. I bet he's warm."

"Next time the captain sends us for him, we should time it so we'd need to spend the night."

"Good thought, but would you feel safe in a cave with him?"

Johnny looked at his friend with a look of consternation and responded, "Do you feel safe anywhere in this war?'

The more time Jason spent alone, the more he thought of Carey and Daniel. Right after his return to camp, he regretted not taking their lives when he had the chance but quickly realized that he would have been just as miserable without her, and the act would have made his own life even more worthless. His homecoming had certainly not been like any of his dreams over the last four years. Instead it had just become another mission infecting him with more guilt and sorrow. After listening to the stories of the soldiers on the ground, looking directly into the eyes of the enemy, fighting to death in hand-to hand-combat, his guilt at what he had been sent to do would triple. The current of sadness that ran through him would be overwhelming. On days like this, the sense of loss would push him into the depths of despair, and he would spend the day in self-loathing.

Jason was awakened by voices.

"Hello, the cave!" shouted Jim.

"He probably has a rifle trained on us, watching since we started climbing."

"Least we didn't get lost again," scoffed Jim.

Jason slowly got to his feet and started toward the cave entrance. The two Missouri boys would be welcome company. When he stepped into the chilling outside air, Jim and Johnny were studying the sky.

Jason lifted his gaze and said, "That's going to be a big storm. What brings you boys up here so late in the day?"

"Captain says you need to be in camp. Some people from Washington want to meet up with you."

Jason surveyed the sky again and said, "You fellas come on in. I don't think we would make it to camp tonight."

As the three soldiers entered the cave, snow began to fall.

HOME

Jason covered the entrance with a make shift door he had fashioned from branches and invited the two soldiers to follow him back into the cave. The passage back was so narrow, Jim and Johnny had to turn sideways to fit through holding their bedrolls in front of their bodies. Jason had found this chamber recently just in time for the cold weather. It was farther under the mountain and had been used by someone before him; it was large enough to accommodate all of them, and whoever the previous inhabitants were had punched a smoke hole to the outside.

Jim saw the fire and said, "I told you he would be warm, but this is downright cozy!"

Jason responded, "Yeah, I'd been in and out of here for six months before I ventured down that passage and discovered this. I guess it was probably a Cherokee hide out."

Johnny laughed and said, "Now it's a soldier's haven. I'm glad we came."

For the second time, Jason realized this cave had become his home and these boys were his guests. He passed around a small jug of shine that the old man from the ferry had given him. As the jug passed, the boys from Missouri relaxed, and the conversation centered around what everyone planned to do when this war ended.

Jim asked, "Will you be heading home?"

Jason thought for a moment and then answered, "I got nothing to go home to. Family's all gone."

Johnny looked up from the fire and said, "You should go to St. Louis with us."

"What a great idea. If you go with us, maybe we won't get lost," Jim added.

Jason laughed and said, "Surely you boys can find your own way home."

"Only if they put us on a train. Over land we'd be lost and starve to death before we found Missouri. Remember, we couldn't even find your cave that first time."

"That's right, Jason. You could be our guide and maybe teach us a little mountain knowledge and survival technique."

"If you're just going back to the city, why would you need survival techniques?" Jason asked.

"We are planning to go west and claim ourselves some land, maybe be cattlemen or even farmers," Jim exclaimed.

"Farmers, huh. I had a farm in a beautiful mountain cove, but I can't go back."

Both the younger soldiers detected the sadness that crept over Jason's face, but neither of them wanted to ask why. They were not sure they wanted to hear about it, whatever it meant. Instead the men said their good nights and, warm in their blankets for the first time since the first of November, slept soundly through the night.

*****

Johnny thought he was at home in his mother's kitchen when he smelled bacon cooking. He rolled over to see Jim hovered over the fire.

He reached for his tin cup, filled it with something that resembled coffee, took a few sips, and said, "Where's Jason?"

"Getting some snow to melt down for water and making some sort of snowshoes to help us hike back to camp. You know he really does have survival instincts that he will teach us."

"Snowshoes?"

"That's right. Last night's storm was a blizzard, three feet of snow and huge drifts."

Johnny sighed and thought hiking in the snow and leaving the warmth of this cave was the last thing he wanted to do. He could get real comfortable here. He also knew that overnight would not cause alarm, but Captain Black had expected them last night. The blizzard would be an excuse for their absence, and Jason had agreed to guide them back to St. Louis when the war ended. It all made him feel almost safe again. He just had to stay alive; surely the conflict could not go on much longer.

Jason had crawled and dug his way out of the cave at dawn. The storm had turned the outside world into a wonderland. The snow had accumulated on the limbs of every tree thicker than two inches.

It was a clean white landscape stretching as far as he could see. It gave Jason hope. Mother Nature's hand had hidden the scars of war on the land; perhaps something could be done about the scars on his heart. He thought of Carey one last time and decided to look to the next chapter of his life; he would go westward with his newest friends.

Jason returned to the inner chamber and said, "We'll have our breakfast and head down to talk to the captain's Washington people. I sure hope it's not an assignment that will take me away from here for long."

The three soldiers secured the cave. Jason wiped away any signs that led to the passage into the back of the cave, hopeful that any marauders that might chance upon the place would not find his food stores. He refilled the hole they crawled through to the outside with snow, standing back satisfied that someone would have to be very observant to find the entrance. Jim and Johnny were waiting for directions; the snow-covered land already had them concerned, for they had no idea which way was the way to the path down to the river.

Jason saw their looks and said, "All right, your education begins now. Where's the river?"

"Ah, gone," replied Jim.

"Use your eyes," Jason said. "Where is the ribbon of smooth snow?"

"There," Johnny pointed in the direction of the river. "I can just see the outline of the ferryboat tied at the landing."

"Good, always look for what is out of place. So if that's the river, which way to the path?"

"Over here," Jim said and started in the right direction. Jason took point since he was most familiar with the steep path, and they made their way down. At the road along the river, Jason pointed out the edge of the ice, and with their snowshoes in place, they trudged through the deep snow in the direction of the encampment. Each soldier lost in their thoughts, they walked in silence

*****

It was January 1865.

Captain Black asked Jason to join him and his guests for dinner in the officers' mess. He was very apprehensive about the meeting; the scuttlebutt around camp was that the men from Washington were part of the Pinkerton Agency. Jason was not sure he wanted to be interviewed by these guys; assassinations were not part of his plan. He only wanted to stay alive until the war ended. The other talk about camp was Sherman's gift of the city of Savannah to President Lincoln. The southern rebellion seemed to be winding down.

The soldiers were all talking about returning home in the spring; according to President Lincoln himself, "Grant had the bear by the hind legs while Sherman was taking off the hide." The future was looking promising; his decision to leave his past behind actually seemed to be coming to the forefront. The idea of guiding the boys to their home and seeing the west was in reach.

Jason sat down at the table with the gentlemen from Washington. The taller of the two men introduced himself as an agent of the Pinkerton Agency.

"We have heard wonderful things about your marksmanship, son," he said slowly, beginning his spiel.

Jason answered, "Yes, sir, but I'm not interested in killing for the Secret Service."

"Hold on there, soldier. You got me wrong. We're looking for a protection detail. We need soldiers with your skills that are trustworthy and true to the cause. The war is ending. The celebration in Washington will be huge and potentially dangerous for the leaders of our country."

"So you are offering me a job?"

"Yes."

"Does it pay better than my present job?"

"Well, yes, considerably more."

"Is there a catch?"

"Well, you will leave with us tomorrow for Washington. And when the surrender comes, you will not be released from service until a later date. Your homecoming will be delayed."

"I wasn't going home. I was going west with some friends."

"Does that mean you are ready to go with us?"

Jason slowed his thoughts like he did before pulling the trigger and said, "Are we ridin' or walkin'?"

"On the train first thing tomorrow morning, weather permitting," came the reply.

"Okay!" And without another word, Jason stood, saluted, and left the mess in search of the Missouri boys.

He found them huddled under a poorly constructed lean-to that faced north. Jason crept close to the structure and pulled out one of the supporting poles, collapsing the structure on top of his two comrades. Jim and Johnny emerged out from under the debris, swearing loudly and ready for a fight. When they saw the sniper, they stopped dead in their tracks, unable to speak.

"Lesson number two, never build a shelter facing the north wind, and make sure your supports are tied to one another so the wind can't blow it down," Jason said with a sneer.

"We weren't expecting you. Show us how to rebuild and maybe we will share our dinner with you," Jim said sheepishly.

Jason laughed.

"You bet. What's for dinner?"

"We was thinking you would share that stew you packed down from the cave."

"Caught that, did ya? Your observation skills are already improving." Jason added, "Plus potatoes from the officer's mess."

At that Johnny jumped up, saluted mockingly, and exclaimed, "How do we begin, sir?"

Jason instructed Johnny to gather some pine boughs and find two forked trees that looked like a Y, at least five feet in height. Then he told Jim to start a fire to thaw the stew and add the potatoes. When Johnny returned with the Y trees, Jason sent him back for several long limbs to be used for ribs. Using the original ridgepole from their makeshift hut, he built a basic three-sided pyramid with one long side. The spot that the boys had chosen was high enough that the ground was dry, and by adding a lot of debris, leaves, and pine boughs, Jason created a sleeping space about three feet deep that would be warm and dry. They added debris on top of the limbs above and sat down for their meal.

After dinner Jason explained about his new job and asked the Missouri boys if they would wait for him at the cave to return after the surrender. They all agreed to meet at the cave after the surrender; no one was willing to voice the fear that they might not make it. Jason began to formulate a plan for traveling cross country with these two; it gave his future some purpose. They crawled inside their shelter, used the only remaining piece of the original lean-to as a door, spread their bedrolls, and amazingly, the three of them slept comfortably through the freezing night.

CHAPTER EIGHTEEN

Jason

After arriving in Washington, Jason had been settled in a room at a downtown boarding house near the Capitol building. Washington was more than a frontier town but not as elaborate as the descriptions of St. Louis from Jim and Johnny. Every morning he would report in at the headquarters of the Union Intelligence Service, the brainchild of Alan Pinkerton.

January, February, and March, Jason wandered the streets of Washington, familiarizing himself with the layout of the city. His superiors were preparing for the culmination of the war; the Union was prevailing. Jason was better acquainted with Washington's layout than most natives. In his wanderings, he had found a game trail leading down to the Potomac River that had become his place of solitude and relaxation. He could move freely throughout the city because of his credentials, so he spent at least an hour a day, sitting at the base of a tree near the river. It brought back memories of his mountains, sometimes painful, but remembering a time before all the killings helped him maintain some of his self-worth and gave him strength.

When he arrived at headquarters the morning of April 14, 1865, the office was in an uproar. President Lincoln had finally signed into law a piece of legislation that would create the Secret Service Division of the Treasury Department. Its primary function was to protect the US currency from counterfeiters and also to defend the president from assassination. Jason was relieved to find out he would be on a protective detail after all and not doing surveillance or undercover work, both of which he found dishonest. He was given his first formal leave since arriving in Washington, a full five-day pass. Jason walked through town in silence, consciously blocking out the sounds and sights of the city. He went back to his room, gathered most of his camping gear, and planned to spend the next five days down by the Potomac River alone. He wanted to get up in the mountains, but even though he had a pass, he didn't think going beyond the army barricade around Washington was worth the chances of getting caught in a skirmish of some kind. The war was definitely winding down, but hostilities continued. Jason walked toward the river, pushed Carey out of his thoughts, and started planning his trip west with the St. Louis boys.

CHAPTER NINETEEN

Jim

Jim sat alone in Jason's cave; he had been there for at least a week. The war had ended for him the day Johnny had died. It had started as a routine patrol and ended in tragedy. Captain Black had ordered them to march out of the small fort they had occupied for the last three years toward Romney to check out a rumor of enemy activity; there had been very little activity since Jason had left for Washington, but it was April, and the melting of the snow had brought back the raiders. Jim had a bad feeling as they marched out of camp, fourteen men on foot and Captain Black on horseback leading the way.

"Stay alert," he whispered to Johnny. They were close to the ferry crossing when it happened. They were ambushed. Captain Black's horse was the first causality. The captain was trying to free himself when he died, shot between the eyes. All the soldiers were running for the cover of trees. Jim looked over his shoulder and saw men falling in the road. The snipers had total advantage. Turning back Jim yelled, "Run, Johnny!" the words had barely cleared his throat when a bullet struck Johnny between the shoulder blades. Jim, still running, caught him as he fell and carried him into the trees. As Jim laid him on the ground, the life drained away. The woods were quiet when the sound of the galloping horses and Rebel yells faded; the marauders rode away.

Jim stood and surveyed the road, looking for a sign of movement among the bodies. There was none.

Jim had no idea how he ended up in Jason's cave. He didn't remember walking or climbing up to the opening, but here he was after a week, sitting, staring at the fire pit. He had to formulate a plan; technically, he was a deserter. He could be shot on sight. The cave was not well-known; he and Johnny were the last visitors. If he was careful, he could just wait for the war's end and Jason's return.

CHAPTER TWENTY

Jason

Jason settled down by the river. He had found a naturally protected spot in an oak grove. The ancient oaks provided enough shelter from the light snowfall that he could sit out by his small fire and enjoy the solitude of the old woods. He leaned back against a tree and fell back into his own self to that place before the war where things were clear. He avoided thoughts of anything after he left for Charleston; in fact, he strayed way back to his childhood memories. He had just conjured up a young Carey by the creek when a voice brought him back from his meditations abruptly.

"Show your hands. Get up! Slowly," the voice demanded.

Jason shook his head to clear the cobwebs and looked up at the soldier standing over him. At Jason's stare, he backed up but remained cautious and defensive, pointing his rifle at Jason's chest. Jason calmly said, "What's wrong, soldier?"

"Show me some kind of identification." And then he added, "Slowly use your left hand."

Jason chuckled to himself said, "Mistake, I am left-handed."

He carefully reached inside his coat, withdrew his papers, and handed them to the soldier.

The soldier relaxed visibly and said, "Sorry, but we have orders to check everyone."

Jason said, "Why, what's happened?"

The soldier's response made Jason flinch with disbelief. He said, "The president's been shot!"

"Is he dead?' came Jason's response.

"It sounded like a fatal wound, but there's been no official word. I can escort you back through town if you want."

"No," Jason said a little too quickly. "I'm off duty for five more days, and I'll be right here if anybody's looking for me."

The soldier backed away and left. Jason wanted to go back to his meditations but realized it was pointless. He figured, as soon as his whereabouts were reported, someone would come for him. When no one had come as the sun set, he crawled into the tent and closed his eyes. He dreamed of the end to all hostilities and returning to the mountains. For the next three days, Jason enjoyed the solitude of his oak grove. He cleaned his rifle and tried to clear his head. Lincoln's death would either accelerate the South's efforts or end the war in favor of the Union. No matter which, he could begin planning his travel west with the St. Louis boys.

On April 17, the same soldier who had confronted him three days earlier walked into his camp and said, "Mr. Emerson, you need to return to the intelligence headquarters as soon as possible."

"Why'd it take you three days to get back here?"

"When I reported your whereabouts, they said not to bother you, but now it's different."

"President Lincoln died?"

"Yes, but they need you because Lee surrendered. Headquarters needs you and the others to guard President Johnson."

CHAPTER TWENTY-ONE

Jim

The water supplies in the cave were running low, and Jim knew that he would be forced to venture outside to find the spring that Jason had mentioned during one of their previous discussions. He had said it was near his sniper perch above the ferry, which was not more than three hundred yards from the cave but well hidden. Jim would not need to go down to the river for the water. If he had thought about this before he could have brought Johnny with him, desertion could have kept them both alive until Jason returned. This thought rushed in on him, and Johnny's brutal death overwhelmed him. He lowered the canteen to the floor of the cave and wept; he had left Johnny's body by the road to protect himself. When the bodies were found, he would be listed as missing in action or captured. He knew he needed to survive and stay hidden; this war would not go on forever, and Jason promised to return.

For the first time since his arrival, the morning was fresh, and there was still a coolness in the air; the view of the valley made him glad to be alive. He started in the direction of the ferry, crossing along the mountainside; his only hope was to stumble onto the spring. He counted his steps, trying not to lose altitude as he followed a game trail in what he hoped was the right direction. A hundred steps later, he heard the sound of the stream and, following it uphill, found the spring. The water problem was solved.

Jim noticed a narrow path that led away and down from the spring. He could leave his canteens at the stream and do a little exploring. The path ended on a small ledge. There was just enough room for one man to sit back against the mountain. He sat down and found himself looking through the tree line at the ferry crossing below. Looking to the left, he saw a forked branch it resembled the Y branches that Jason had cut for the lean-to. Jim thought, *That's interesting. This branch is cut in the same manner.* Suddenly it came to him. This was where the "sniper" had been, who killed the home guard on the ferry. Jason had been the shooter. In the next moment, Jim was thinking of Johnny again; the snipers that had massacred his patrol the week before were hidden in places like this. They were murderers; he was waiting for a murderer. Johnny was dead because of men like Jason.

A movement at the ferry landing caught Jim's attention. He let all those disturbing thoughts fade and concentrated on trying to hear what the rider was yelling about. The sound drifted up to his perch; he couldn't trust his hearing; the news was so startling.

"President Lincoln's been killed," followed by, "Lee surrendered at Appomatox." Apparently, the ferry operator didn't believe his ears either because Jim heard the man yell it a second time. This time it was clear, and the meaning of it was even clearer—the war was over.

Jim fell back onto the mountain rest, covering his own mouth with his hands to stifle the shout of joy that was trying to escape. It was over; he could go home. But because of his desertion, Jim had to formulate a plan to get back into the fort. It was simple; he could just walk into camp. It would be his secret. He only needed a viable explanation for the last seven days.

The following day, he wandered into the area of the fort. The perimeter guards confronted him.

"Who goes there? State your business?"

Lucky for Jim, one of the soldiers who knew him yelled, "It's Jim! He survived the ambush."

Jim had no need for an explanation; the soldiers provided it for him.

"Look at his head."

Jim remembered how he must appear, covered in mud and blood; maybe he was concussed after all. He had made no effort to clean away Johnny's blood. The guards took him directly to the new commanding officer to report. The man in charge was a young Lieutenant Sorrenson, Jim had never even seen him before.

"Tell me what happened. Captain Black was found under his horse. He never even fired his gun."

Jim recounted the ambush, breaking down when he described the scene on the road after Johnny had died in his arms. Lieutenant Sorrenson listened quietly and seemed to believe the lie that came after. Jim told him he awoke disoriented and walked into the woods in the wrong direction, getting farther from the fort. His reputation for getting lost in the woods saved him; no one doubted his story. Sorrenson dismissed him and sent him to the infirmary to get cleaned up and await his discharge. He would even have mustering-out pay to contribute to his travel expenses.

Jim felt a great relief as he walked out of the lieutenant's tent, but he was completely unprepared for the reaction of the soldiers in his extended company. They cheered him like a hero.

CHAPTER TWENTY-TWO

Jason

Jason had quickly gathered his belongings and made his way back into Washington proper. The streets were already filling with celebrators; the War Between the States was over. Of course, it would be days before all the armies in the field could be notified, and what if General Meade's armies were still fighting? Jason worked his way through the gathering crowds to the building housing the office of the Intelligence Agency.

When he walked in, he was greeted from every direction.

"Where have you been?"

"Did you hear?"

"Time to go to work. No more hanging around down by the river, soldier," said Michael with a good-hearted smile.

"Just preparing mentally for what's ahead," Jason answered back.

"Crowd control without sidearms sounds like fun, but you'll be in a tree somewhere."

The mental image of his first ambush and Nathan's cousin rushed in so fast, he had to turn away quickly to get control. He walked down the hall; Michael followed at a distance. When he turned back toward him, Michael backed away, saying, "Jason, are you all right?"

Jason knew he was looking at Michael, but the face he saw was Nathan's. He shook his head, and the vision faded.

"Of course I'm all right," he answered, but he knew it was a lie. He had hoped that his time in the woods would help with the flashbacks, but he was wrong. He would need to watch for what triggered them. Michael had seen the anger; the fear in his face indicated that Jason actually had to struggle not to lash out in that instant. He had heard stories from combat soldiers about fits of anger during rest, but why was he being affected this way? Carey had always been his anchor; without her he was no longer grounded. He would have to get through the next few weeks without any incidents.

"Sorry, Michael," he said as he walked away.

Michael watched him go and wondered what the problem with Jason could be; he was normally mild mannered and quiet. He didn't know him well; as far as he could tell, no one knew him. He shrugged and went back to work, planning the day's itinerary for the Grand Review. Jason would have a very small, probably totally unnecessary job those two days.

Jason could view almost the full length of Pennsylvania Avenue from his position on the roof of the Treasury Building. Every building along the route for the Grand Review had watchers and snipers like himself posted. Jason found the volleys of thunder, not cannon fire, and the rain through the night had enhanced his stress for the job ahead. No one really believed there could be an attack directed toward President Johnson, and yet here he was with a loaded rifle pointed toward the area approaching the timber platform on the lawn of the president's home.

It was early in the morning, and already, thousands of spectators were gathering along Pennsylvania Avenue, on rooftops, in windows, and leaning over balconies for a better view of the street. Jason scanned with his scope and found other snipers on rooftops and civilians clinging to trees and lampposts and even telegraph poles.

He found it amusing and depressing; none of these people could remotely understand what the men they were about to honor had been through. Private homes and public buildings were adorned with evergreen boughs and flags snapped in the May breeze. Children released from school assembled on the north end of the Capitol to catch glimpses of the Army of the Potomac forming up for one final march behind the purple silk headquarters flag of General Meade.

Jason turned back to his assigned watch area, he noticed the American flag flew at full staff for the first time since Lincoln's death. General Grant and President Johnson stood side by side along with several other dignitaries. Jason had been told that Meade and Sherman would be joining them as well. Jason had to remind himself that his job was to watch, not to kill, but it would have been easy; these people were the reason he had left his home in the mountains to become a part of this awful war. He wondered how they would feel if they knew they were being protected by a West Virginian, the state that had been formed after the war, with many mixed loyalties and debated politics.

Now that the procession had begun, Jason would spend the next six hours concentrating on the immediate position of President Johnson and his guests. The soldiers filed by with the effortless discipline mastered on a hundred previous marches. Something caught Jason's eye—a galloping horse. He swung his rifle and scope away from the president, recognized the flowing hair of Custer, and knew this was not a threat. If anything, it was a stunt for more attention by this brazen young general; he was faking a runaway. How absurd.

At the end of the day, Jason climbed down from his perch and walked down the steps of the Treasury Building. He stopped and looked back at the building; it was adorned with flowers and a sign that read "The only national debt we can never repay is the debt we owe our victorious Union soldiers."

"And their families and their loved ones will never be paid either," he said aloud to himself and headed home to spend another restless night as a Union soldier. Tomorrow he would be back on his perch, but each day brought him closer to release and the West. He only hoped that Jim and Johnny would be waiting for him at the cave.

Walking back to his hotel, he passed by many of the same men who had marched down Pennsylvania Avenue; they were mostly getting drunk. Some staggered along, obviously under the influence of laudanum. Their final performance of the war was over; they were officially civilians. The only purpose they had was to forget. Jason realized, at that moment, he was glad he was not going home. These men who had learned how to kill and maim would be taking on a mighty task to return home to lives so changed.

Overnight Washington was inundated with even more parade observers; they all came to see the survivors and heroes of the war. Today, the victorious western armies, who had marched from Atlanta to the sea, would stroll down Pennsylvania Avenue. Jason watched the long, loose stride of these tattered and lean soldiers and sensed the strength and devotion they must have had to follow Sherman across enemy territory. He also sensed their mood; there was a current of sadness throughout. These men knew that marching alongside them were the ghosts of three more soldiers that would never return home. This parade was the last ordered task of the awful ordeal from which they were only too glad to get away.

Jason watched as the final stage of the parade appeared and passed by the viewing stand. The "bummers," as they were known, consisted of scavengers and some freed slaves with their families. These were the men—some soldiers, some not—who preceded Sherman's army. Most of what this branch of the army did was irregular and punishable, but Sherman allowed them to finish out the parade with honor. They were ahead of the skirmish line and greatly contributed to Sherman's unimpeded progress. They reminded Jason of his own somewhat-irregular services, and he was also looking forward to the end of that service.

When he left his perch the second day, Jason went directly to the riverfront. He flopped down under the trees, shook away the memories of his missions, and stared at the leaves and discarded flowers floating with the current. He slowly felt the tension fade away and once again reaffirmed that his purpose was to get to the cave. He only hoped that his discharge would not be delayed for long.

Michael was greatly relieved that the ordeal of the Grand Review was over. Now he started organizing the men under his command for their after-war details. When he came to Jason Emerson, he hesitated; their confrontation from the week before had left him with a bad feeling. He really didn't think Jason could continue on the protection detail or even in the peacetime Secret Service; he was displaying emotional problems.

He learned from others at the office that Jason had demonstrated similar outbursts like the one he had witnessed, some that had led to actual violence, and afterward Jason didn't even remember. When he researched his background, he discovered how many sharpshooter missions he had successively completed before coming to Washington. He was highly decorated, but Jason needed some down time. Michael believed it would take months for him to return to normal; Jason had definitely been damaged by his work. The stress of protecting the president would be too much for his fragile condition. His recommendation was that he be immediately discharged with honors and with pay. Jason was overwhelmed when Michael handed him his discharge papers. Michael could see the emotion in Jason's eyes.

"Go home, soldier. No more killing," Michael said quietly.

"I have no home to go back to," Jason answered with a sadness that Michael could barely understand.

Jason understood the implications of returning to civilian life. Most soldiers would never be the same again, and someone like him was lost in the blackness of his own soul. Jason knew he had been used by the Union, and now that he was damaged goods, they were throwing him to the wolves, but even if going home wasn't a choice, he would have to overcome the rage or at least learn to control it. Jason felt lucky to have comrades who would be at least understanding of his plight, waiting for him. He would leave for Romney and the cave immediately. The trains were crowded with departing soldiers, so Jason bought a horse and started overland to Romney and the cave.

Jason rode along the Potomac River bank out of Washington; it was pleasant under the trees, and there was no foot traffic. The roads were crowded with local soldiers heading to homes outside of Georgetown and even as far as Leesburg. The distances made waiting for a train tedious; they could get there quicker walking. Jason began to realize how lucky he was to have had a government job at the end. He could afford a horse, and he left with rations. Leaving the riverbank, he observed way more empty sleeves and ill-fitting wooden legs as he slowly rode north toward the crossing at Leesburg. He could see the guilt, sorrow, and purposelessness in the eyes of these returning soldiers. Some of them appeared to be suspended between the dead and the living. He felt anger at what had happened to them all, and it was made even more depressing by the fact that these men were the victorious.

He pushed to get through Leesburg before the night overtook him. He camped on the south fork of the Shenandoah River in a wooded area that showed the remains of an encampment, probably occupied by a Union company. It made starting a fire easier, but Jason was unable to sleep comfortably; his mind played tricks on him. He awakened several times; sure, there were snipers in the trees, and they all had his own face. By early dawn, he was ready to ride on.

The closer he came to Winchester, the more he saw signs of battles fought; he didn't remember who the winners were at Opequon Creek. He wasn't sure if it was real or imagined, but the soil seemed reddened by the blood of men who had fallen here. He began to think about all the murders, his murders; how could he chase the death out of his head when it was all around him? Hopefully, when he and the boys hopped on a riverboat in Cincinnati, they could leave the war behind.

The countryside outside of Winchester was less war ravaged. The tree-lined road was pleasant traveling, and his spirits rose as he realized he would make the cave near Romney before nightfall. Even if the boys had moved on, he could get a good night's sleep and prepare to go west.

CHAPTER TWENTY-THREE

Jason and Jim

Day to day at the cave, Jim had developed a routine. He had taught himself as much as he could about finding his way in the woods. He remembered that Jason said it was all about observing, picking landmarks and assigning them an easily remembered name that went with the description. He had managed to leave his camp in every directions and find his way back without getting lost. Jim felt that for a city boy, he was doing well.

He had given Jason a deadline. If he didn't show up by tomorrow, he was going to head for Cincinnati on his own. He could always follow the railroad track if he didn't trust himself. Jim straightened up the cave, putting things away, storing any food that would keep; he felt it was important to leave it like he had found it—mainly in case Jason came back, but some other weary soldier might stumble into this safe refuge.

He debated whether to leave a message for Jason but, in the end, thought it better not to. Jim had just put the last freshly killed rabbit he had on the spit when he heard someone approaching. He reached across the fire, retrieved his rifle, and quietly laid it across his lap.

"Hello, the cave," Jason yelled. "Can I approach?"

Jim leaped to his feet dropping the rifle and rushed through the narrow passage to the entrance of the cave. The two men stood face-to-face, not quite knowing how to react. After a full minute of awkward silence, Jason extended his hand to Jim. Jim grabbed the hand and pulled Jason into a big hug; much to his surprise, Jason accepted the display of emotion willingly. When they separated and backed away, a little embarrassed, Jason smiled and said, "Where's Johnny?"

The expression on Jim's face was the answer. Jason knew instinctively Johnny was among the fallen. He couldn't bring himself to ask how it had happened; instead he followed Jim silently through the narrow passage, and the men ate the rabbit and said their good nights.

Jason was exhausted from the day's travel but was unable to sleep for several hours. He knew that Johnny's death had been a violent one. He hoped that Jim would be able to share the story, but he wasn't willing to push it.

On the opposite wall of the cave, Jim struggled to keep his anger under control. He knew he was being irrational; Jason was not in a tree the day Johnny died, but some other fool whose friend had died could be having these same thoughts. His feelings about the attack were always in his head. At this moment, he thought killing Jason would alleviate some of his guilt. Then, he heard Johnny's voice in his head say, "You should go to St. Louis with us" and his answer, "What a great idea then maybe we won't get lost." He needed Jason to make it home.

The next morning, Jason and Jim organized the cave and carried what they would travel with down the mountain to where Jason had left his horse hobbled in a meadow near a creek that ran to the river. The horse had not wandered too far, so they easily shifted the pack around to accommodate Jim's belongings. Jim watched as Jason expertly adjusted the pack to make it ride properly on the horse's back and thought of another skill that would be helpful in the West. Walking together, leading the horse, they started along the river then turned onto the Grafton road.

"Hey, Jim, how would you feel about catching a boat ride in Parkersburg? I've actually never traveled by boat."

"Boats are all right. It sure beats walking. I'm already tired. But don't forget, you are going to educate me about the navigation in the woods," Jim responded.

Jason laughed and said, "There will be plenty of places to get you lost before we get to the Ohio. It's going to take three days, I reckon. It's 150 miles."

"I imagine a boat will look mighty good after that kinda walkin'. We better get to it!"

They trudged on mostly in silence, each man lost in his own thoughts. When they reached a crossroads where a crude wooden sign pointed left to Carrick's Fork, they decided to stop for the night. They walked about a hundred yards into the woods and set up camp. Dinner was leftover rabbit from the night before and some onions they found near the road, just growing wild. Jason had coffee that he had carried with him from Washington.

"This is good coffee. I haven't had any real coffee since I left home," Jim announced.

"How long you been gone from St. Louis?" Jason asked.

Jim leaned back against a tree and thought for a few minutes. Jason could see he was going back in his memory to before the war. Those times seemed so long ago and, at the same time just a moment ago.

When Jim spoke, it was mournful.

"Johnny and I enlisted in 1862, but we didn't leave the St. Louis area until '63. They put us on the Ohio and Mississippi Rail Road all the way to Cincinnati, Ohio. We had never left Missouri, and before we knew it, we was three states away. It was the damnedest thing, riding in those boxcars with our feet hanging out the door. Of course, we took turns. It was crowded in those cars."

"Johnny talked nonstop about the trains. He was going to be a conductor when the war was over, until he met you. After we met you, all he talked about was going west with your help. Man, he was my best friend, and now he is gone."

Jason looked across the fire when Jim finished that sentence. He was a little taken aback at the look of anger in Jim's eyes. He expected to see tears or a sadness, but this was different and seemed to be directed at him.

Jason said, "What is it? Tell me what happened to Johnny in the end. Were you there?"

"No, I can't talk about it yet."

Jim slung his remaining coffee in the fire and walked out into the darkness. Jason thought it best to leave it alone.

He had things he wouldn't be forced to talk about as well. There was going to be a lot of time between here and St. Louis to share their losses.

They were well on their way to Clarksburg when they came upon a family stranded in the road. The wagon was loaded down with possibly everything they owned. The woman was holding a small child in her arms and trying to keep the rest of her brood from wandering too far.

The older boy, who may have been twelve years old, was helping his father. He couldn't have weighed more than eighty pounds, but he was dedicated to lifting the wagon with a long pole.

Jason and Jim offered to help. When the man walked from around the back of the wagon, the frustration was obvious. He was a wounded veteran with only one leg. He had a crude peg leg attached, but if it wasn't painful enough to walk on it, Jason imagined it would be excruciating to push and lift.

"Here, son. We can do that you help your father," Jason commanded.

The boy looked from Jim to Jason and then to his father with hesitation.

"Do as they say, boy. It's all right."

The four of them quickly had the wheel repositioned, and the wagon was ready to travel.

When the job was completed, the man said, "Thanks, I hope you don't expect payment 'cause we ain't got nothing to give."

Jim quickly answered, "No, sir, you can't pay us. We travelers need to stick together. Where are you headed?"

"Clarksburg, we got kin there."

"We are going to hop on a boat in Parkersburg," Jim said.

Jason stood back contemplating Jim's next move. He wasn't liking the idea of traveling with all these children.

He started to interrupt the conversation but stopped when a small girl grabbed his hand and said, "You can ride with me. My name's Carey."

Jim turned to Jason and said, "Don't that beat all!"

Before Jason recovered from the shock, their pack horse was tied and walking along behind the wagon, and he was sitting next to Carey on the second seat. The boy who had helped with the repair was on the other side of him and the younger boys were in the back with all the belongings. Jim and the father, Jack was his name, walked while Mom, Maryanne, drove, holding the baby across her lap.

The little girl, Carey, babbled on about everything—why they had left their home in Hagerstown, how her daddy had gone off to war and left his leg at a place called Gettysburg. Jason was thankful that she was so busy talking, no one asked him any questions. Besides, Jim was talking almost as much as the girl, so these folks would know everything they would need to know by the time they reached Clarksburg. He did find it strange that Jim's tongue was so loose now since they had not had a conversation longer than a few sentences since they left the cave. However, he was enjoying the ride even if the children were in constant motion.

Jack said, "You boys need to stay with us tonight. My father will make room for us all."

Jim accepted quickly; he knew Jason wanted to push through Clarksburg, but he was thinking a hot meal and a bed sure would be welcome. Jason wanted to object but thought, why push? There was really no reason to hurry as long as they were able to secure a riverboat job before their money and provisions ran out.

The wagon stopped in front of a moderate home a block off Main Street in Clarksburg. The children bolted from the wagon and attacked an elderly man who was holding the gate open for them. He was gruff looking but had only kind words for each child. Then he sent them to the porch, where their grandmother was waiting. He assisted his daughter-in-law from the seat, and Jack handed the baby down to his arms. The joy in his face at seeing his youngest grandson changed his demeanor from gruff to soft.

He laughingly said, "So the family is complete with little Jackson, right?"

"Oh, yes," Maryanne said, "complete." She took the baby and headed to the porch.

Jack climbed down awkwardly; Jason noticed his father did not offer to help, which was of course the right thing to do. He had seen the determination of men who had lost limbs in this war. They did not want pity. They shook hands and then hugged briefly. Then the older gentleman turned his attention to the other two men in the party.

Jack introduced Jim, and then Jason, explaining how they had helped and that he had offered them a place to stay overnight. Jason expected the man to turn them away or at the least send them to the barn.

He looked them over thoughtfully and said, "You boys blue or gray? You know Clarksburg is the birthplace of Stonewall Jackson."

Jason squared his shoulders and said very matter-of-factly, "I fought to save the Union."

Jim hesitated and then said, "Me too."

The old man considered their answers and announced, "Well, I guess we saved it, but I'm not sure it came out too well for either side. Thank the good Lord it is over!"

"Amen to that," said Jim, and the four men walked across the small yard.

They sat on the porch and talked about all that had happened since Jack had left his home. He talked of the battle at Gettysburg and how lucky he had been to only lose his leg and not his life. Jim told a little about his stay outside of Romney. When they turned to hear Jason's story, he quickly changed the subject to riverboats. The subject brought a twinkle to Jack's father, and he told story after story about piloting boats up and down the Ohio before the war.

When he slowed down enough to interrupt, Jason asked, "Any chance you can help us get work on a boat headed to Cincinnati?"

"So you boys are headed west? How far?"

Jim said, "I'm heading home to St. Louis and then west. Jason here came along so I wouldn't get lost." Then he laughed and looked at Jason with the crooked smile that Jason remembered from the early cave days.

He is such a kid, Jason thought.

"Yes, sir," Jason said. "We hoped we could hire on as far as Cincinnati and then strike out cross-country. So I can teach Jim here some wood skills to be better prepared for the frontier."

"You know the railroad runs all the way to St. Louis."

"Yep," said Jim. "That's how I got to Cincinnati, but I need skills for trapping and such to go where I plan to go."

"Well, you are in luck. I talk with an old friend that still runs the river regularly. I can send you with letters. He has been hiring a lot of veterans for that trip."

Jason exchanged looks with Jim, and they both answered together with a resounding "Thanks!"

The dinner that followed was the first time Jim and Jason had sat around a table family-style since before the war. The family joined hands, and Jack's father thanked the Lord for allowing him to have his family safe under his roof again. Jason stared across the table at little Carey and only saw his own Carey and allowed himself to once again think of how this was the life they should have had. Jim thought of Johnny and couldn't stop the anger even when he noticed the tenderness in Jason's eyes. Jason noticed the intensity in Jim's face and thought, *Whatever is going on with Jim, we will eventually need to confront.* He was beginning to expect it had to do with Johnny's death and, of course, the war. His own flashbacks and disturbing dreams had begun to wane the farther from Washington and West Virginia that he walked, but he heard Jim's calls and screams in his sleep at night.

CHAPTER TWENTY-FOUR

Riverboat Trip

After a full day of steady walking, Jim and Jason camped along a quiet stream within an hour of Parkersburg. They decided it would be best to arrive fresh and ready for work at the docks even if the captain they were looking for might not be headed out on that day. Jack's father had told them they would find Captain Humphreys on the riverboat the *Ohio Patriot*.

At daybreak they broke camp and packed the horse for one more trek. They planned to sell him at the docks, so they packed their personal items and camp gear in separate packs that they could carry on board the vessel. Both men were excited about the possibility of finding work on the *Ohio Patriot*.

It was easy enough to find the docks; apparently, everything going west, including a lot of bedraggled soldiers, were being shipped out on these boats. As they weaved their way along, Jason noticed a lot of men wandering the streets; some appeared drunk but others simply disoriented.

Jim also noticed these men; one in particular caught his eye and he called out, "Mark Johnson, is it you?"

The soldier who was still in a ragged uniform quickly stood at attention and called back, "Yes, sir, ready for duty."

Jim approached the man and said, "Don't you know me? It's Jim from home."

The soldier who looked to be old enough to be Jim's father turned away and ran, or rather hobbled away.

"Somebody you knew from before?" Jason asked

"I think so, but why did he run away?"

"I met soldiers on both sides in Washington that no longer know who they are. Not all that served are as lucky as you and me," Jason added. "I think he is lost in battle and can't find any way back."

"Another friend lost," Jim said sadly, and they walked on in silence.

There were several boats docked along the wharf. Jim and Jason easily found the *Ohio Patriot*. They were in luck; she was being loaded, which meant she was making ready for a trip to Cincinnati. However, it probably meant the crew was already hired. They asked one of the dock workers where they could find Captain Humphreys.

"What's your business with the captain?" came the reply.

"We're looking for work. We have letters of introduction to the captain," Jason said with authority.

The man looked Jim and Jason up and down and said, "The captain is down by the stern." He pointed and then added, "Walk that way."

Jim followed Jason, and they walked in the direction they were told. Near the end of the boat was Captain Humphreys. He was a formidable-looking man at least six feet tall. He stood absolutely straight backed and was yelling instructions at a little monkey of a man who was crawling around on the big paddles that pushed the boat forward.

"Can ya see the problem, Jacque?" he shouted.

"Yes, sir," came the reply. The little man's voice was an octave higher than the captain's and sounded excited.

"So can you fix it?" Captain Humphreys yelled with some aggravation.

"Yes, sir, but I'll need a few more hands."

Captain Humphreys looked around and, seeing Jason standing nearby, said, "Get out there and give him a hand."

Jason looked over his shoulder to see who the captain was speaking to. When he realized he was speaking to him, instead of answering, he climbed out on the paddle wheel and offered his assistance.

The little man seemed confused, but he just shrugged and said, "Okay, grab that rod behind you and shove it into that hole at the side there, and keep pushing until I say stop."

Jason did as he was told.

"All right, that did it. Thanks."

They climbed back to the dock. Captain Humphreys thanked them and was walking away when he stopped and turned back to face them.

"Jacque, did you hire this man? I don't recognize him."

"No, sir, but he sure was helpful."

Jim stepped forward and said, "Jason and I came down here to get jobs. We have a letter from Captain John Edwards."

Captain Humphreys's laugh was contagious; he looked at them and said, "Ever worked on a riverboat?"

Jason smiled and said, "I helped a fella fix a big wooden paddle once."

Jim said, "I watched."

"Show me those letters. You boys are in real luck 'cause I need two more men to fill this crew."

Captain Humphreys studied the letters for a few moments, looked up, and announced, "Welcome aboard, gents."

They sold their pack horse, had dinner in town, and spent the night in their new quarters aboard the *Ohio Patriot*. Jason thought living below decks was a lot like living in his cave but way more crowded. The closeness of all these men made it claustrophobic. Jason had not lived among others since early in the war, when his sniper assignments began.

The following morning, they were floating away from the docks at Parkersburg en route to Cincinnati. By midmorning, they had been given their individual duties. Jim felt like he was back in the army, but it somehow settled his nerves to be under someone else's command. Jason was trying to adjust to being in such close contact with people; he did not know or even have inside information about them. He was living with strangers, which was unsettling.

He had been told to assist Jacque. The little man seemed to intuitively understand Jason's quiet, slow-moving temperament, which was in direct odds with his own quick ways. He also quickly picked up on Jason's observation skills and how he measured everything accurately without a mistake. He started pointing out river changes and obstruction in the river and explained how dangerous they were. At one point, he made the comment that observing the river wasn't a lot different from tracking in the woods. Knowing the distance from an obstacle or snag could be really helpful in certain situations. Jason spent any free time he had watching the water. It was fascinating, the ripples, how the water changed directions even though it continued to flow toward Cincinnati. It was somehow peaceful and angry in the same instant, not unlike his own existence.

At night Jason turned in early and listened to the conversations around him but never participated. He hoped Jim would not talk about the circumstances of their friendship; he did not want the war veterans among the crew to think he was a murderer. He was sure there would be men among them who had been the victims of sniper attacks or knew of the killings that he and others like him had committed. There were killings that he felt justified in like the ferryboat assassination, but his early ambushes were nothing more than death dealing at the orders of Union officers. Strategically, they may have been important to the cause, but the dread he felt ate away at his soul.

Every forty miles, the riverboat would make a stop to replenish its fuel. Along the banks of the river, small outposts and sometimes actual towns had developed for the purpose of supplying wood for the steam engines that turned the big stern wheel. The regular crew members that made the trip regularly knew the best stops; some even had girlfriends or wives and families that lived nearby. With the Captain's permission, they would leave the boat and spend time with their families while the rest of the crew labored at loading wood for the boilers. There was always a lot of lighthearted banter about how all you needed for time off was a family. The men leaving the boat for these outings laughed along with the others, but Jason knew they were the lucky ones; they had families and loved ones to join even if just for the day. He noticed that none of the war veterans left the riverboat. Some, of course, were on their way to families at the end of the run; some were going farther west, trying to outrun the memories, not unlike himself.

They reached their next fuel stop ahead of schedule, so the captain gave everyone a twenty-four-hour leave in the small town but instructed the crew that if anyone returned too drunk or hungover to work, they would not be allowed to board.

Jason never left the vessel, realizing this would be his opportunity to have some privacy. Besides Captain Humphreys, Jacque, and two other cargo guards, the boat was empty. Jason carefully unwrapped his rifle and began to break it down. He had been unable to do this for fear someone would recognize its purpose.

He sensed more than heard the intrusion. Captain Humphreys was standing at the bottom of the ship's ladder.

"Sorry," he apologized. "I am in the habit of inspecting these quarters when I know they have been vacated."

Jason shrugged and said, "You are the captain."

Captain Humphreys walked to where Jason was sitting and, peering over his shoulders, said, "I don't pretend to know much about rifles, but that is designed for long-range shooting, yes?"

"Yes," answered Jason.

"You planning to shoot game with that out west?"

"Yes," Jason said slowly.

"Maybe when we get into the shallows, you could shoot us a deer for a good venison meal. Could you hit one off a moving post?"

"Don't know. I've never had to do that. Always been stationary when I fired."

"One of the places that we stop for wood, there's a herd of deer that we pass on the way in. It would be good sport. The fellas could bet on whether you can do it or not. What do ya think?"

"Captain, I don't want them to know who I was in the war. They don't like me much as it is when they know who I really am. Well . . ." Jason trailed off.

Captain Humphreys looked at the young man before him and said, "We have all done things in war that affected us deeply, but the war is over. Don't let yourself or others define you. Put it behind you, and go forward." Then he added, "Let the river carry you. Go with the flow." He climbed the ladder and left Jason alone.

Jason thought about the conversation and finished cleaning his rifle; he added back the silver items that Ethan had removed back in Ohio and began to think about how to prepare for the contest coming up. He walked upon deck, and leaning over the bow of the *Ohio Patriot*, he watched the river flow away from the war in the direction of the future. Jason started calculating the speed of the river; he would need to know how many feet a second the boat would be moving to know where to aim, and if the deer was grazing or moving, the shot would be impossible. This was a marksman's challenge. He and Jim could pool their money and be winners; no one among the crew would believe he could do this.

Members of the crew began to return to the *Patriot* at dinner time. Most of them didn't have money enough for a night on the town anyway. Jim had gone in with a couple of his new buddies from the boiler room, where he slung wood all day. It sounded as if it had been a pleasant day ashore.

When he could, Jason pulled Jim aside and told him about the deer hunt. At first, he seemed keen on the challenge but grew sullen and refused to be directly involved in the practice sessions that Jason had planned. He voiced something about being done with guns and killings. Jason tried to tell him it was hunting, a skill he would need out west, but Jim refused to listen and left him standing alone.

"What's troubling him?" Jacque asked.

Jason just shook his head. Jacque offered to help with the practice; Captain Humphreys had already informed him of the plan. Jason thought Jacque would be helpful; he knew the flow of the river better than anyone, with the exception of the pilot. Jason had forty miles to figure the way to make this kill. He would be on deck night and day since he and Jacque were scouring the river during the next part of the journey for snags and debris and, of course, shallows. At night, by the light of the torch baskets, they watched the river for snags, felled timber, hidden rocks, and sandbars.

Jason asked Jacque, "Why aren't these things charted?"

"The river changes daily, sometimes hourly. It remakes itself."

Jason thought, *That is what I need to do, remake myself, start over, clear my head.*

Captain Humphreys gave Jason permission to fire his rifle when the boat was drifting in nonpopulated areas, so Jason started to understand the difficulty of the shot he would be taking. He tried to remember his father's instructions about shooting from a moving horse. Before he was trained as a sniper, he witnessed the cavalry shooting from their mounts, but he knew if it was a long-distance shot, they always halted and then aimed and fired while standing in their stirrups. There were definite variables to be considered. This was a puzzle that suited his temperament and training.

The crew were starting to speculate; he knew the soldiers among them already suspected his past, and now others aboard were showing their apprehension about him. Only Jacque and the captain seemed unchanged by his new status, but Jim's attitude troubled him the most. The civilian crew were leery of all the veterans; Jason had noticed the farther away from the war zone they ventured, the more fear of what these young men had become was obvious among the common folk. They assumed that once a man had killed daily in battle, he was not fit to return to normalcy around the good folk at home, even if he was one of the victors. Jason had heard of wives who were afraid of their returning husbands and, of course, children who only knew their fathers as soldiers. He was starting to realize he wasn't the only man walking around with deep secrets. Strangely, the contest was helping him see a way to break free of his soldiering and use his skill and training just as a pastime. Let the betting begin.

Whenever the opportunity to stand in one place and observe the riverbank arose, Jason began to sort out the best way to steady his gun. Since the railing moved up and down with the water, he would need to lean against it rather than rest on it. He would not have as long to aim as was his normal procedure because he simply would not be able to hold the gun steady for too long before his arm would give out. Any stationary brace that he devised would have nothing to rest on that didn't move, but if he leaned on the rail and held the gun tight against his shoulder, he could use his upper body as the stationary rest.

Jacque sent him below about 2:00 a.m. each evening to get some sleep before the next watch. Jason lay in his bunk and visualized the act of shooting a deer—no, shooting a buck—from the deck of the *Ohio Patriot*. He could see the herd as the boat rounded the bend described to him by Jacque. When the landing bell rang, they would startle and move away along the bank. The buck would lag behind as his does moved off. Jason would be ready when he moved into the opening and establish a point ahead of his motion and fire. In his visualization, the deer would gallop on a few strides and then drop in full view of the crew—a heroic shot that would provide fresh meat for everyone, showcase his skill, and give it a positive spin for his future. His last job as a soldier was to protect President Johnson; his first job as a civilian would be to feed his companions. It provided him with hope for his blackened soul; maybe someone would see him as a worthwhile human being instead of a murderer.

Though unwilling to be a part of Jason's preparation, Jim watched whenever he was on deck. It bothered him that he felt so much pent-up rage against Jason the sniper; inside he knew it was unfair to think of him as Johnny's killer. He didn't fight for the Rebels, but his method of fighting made him the enemy. As he watched him calculate and learn how to follow the motion of the river, his intensity that revolved around making this one shot taught him why Jason was so good at observation—the same observation skills that he had wished to learn all those months ago at the cave. In this thought, Jim understood that the men who had killed his friend were not sharpshooters like Jason; they were cowards who hunted from treetops like carrion birds and were simply lucky to have killed a group of running men.

In order for Jason to understand how he felt and forgive how he had been acting, he would need to tell Jason how Johnny had died. Jim still wasn't sure he could talk about it with anyone, but he did know that he needed to talk with Jason about it before they started toward St. Louis. Once they started across the outback areas, they would need to watch each other's backs. He could not expect Jason to prepare him for continuing west if he continued to mistrust him. He needed to act normally.

That evening Jason approached Jim about the upcoming deer hunt and the onboard gambling that had started. He wanted them to be a part of it but had hesitated to talk with Jim because of the tension between them. He found Jim leaning over the aft rail alone.

"Hey there," Jason hailed Jim as he walked toward him along the deck. "We need to talk."

Jim turned in the direction of Jason's approach and said rather flatly, "We do."

Jason stopped in his tracks, a little unsure of how to react when Jim launched into the story of how Johnny had died at the hands of some Rebel sharpshooters. Jason listened to every word without interruption; his insides were churning from the guilt that devoured him. These men who had killed Jim's childhood friend were men trained like him. He had known there were Confederate sharpshooters, but he himself had only been in three ambushes that were similar to what he was hearing. They also were massacres, and after he had seen those men fall by his hand, he could have killed more, but after his third shot, he couldn't make himself load again. He remembered Captain Black was furious with him, but he didn't care. He would fire his three key shots usually at officers and walk away. It was the beginning of his soldiering as a selective assassin. It was what led to the Washington job in the long run, and he was able to justify what he was doing.

He looked at Jim and said, "If I could erase the memory of every killing that I contributed to in the war, I would gladly, but instead I will see them until I die. I will understand if you don't want to be around me for another second."

"I came to realize watching you prepare for this deer hunt that you are not a random killer like the men who ended Johnny. I can forgive you for what you did as a soldier. My anger at you was because of what I did. I lived. I deserted my best friend. He died on the side of a road."

Jim leaned on the railing of the boat and wept. Jason's first instinct was to say something that might explain how none of the deaths in the war were any one man's fault, but the words wouldn't come. He put his hand on Jim's shoulder and said, "Captain Humphreys told me, 'Let the river carry you. Go with the flow.' Maybe you could try to go forward from here, forgive yourself, and please forgive me."

Jason took his hand away and started to walk down the deck. Jim lifted his head and followed him. Jason looked over his shoulder and said, "Catch up. I need to tell you the plan for killing this deer and makin' some money."

Jim didn't let himself hesitate; this was the direction away from the war's memories, and he intended to put it behind him. In three days' time, the boat would be approaching the fuel stop and the landing where they would be having venison dinner. Jim told Jason he could handle the betting side of things; he should just concentrate on making the shot.

"Are we betting for or against my shot?" Jason said.

"I've never seen you fire a rifle, but I'm betting that we eat venison," Jim said. "I think a side bet is the way to make out the best."

After their talk, things between Jason and Jim returned to the original cave days except for Johnny's absence, but now when he was mentioned, they could talk about the good memories. Jim talked on and on about St. Louis and the places he and Johnny used to visit. Jason learned why they had fought and all of their plans for after the war. They began to talk about their own future plans. They discussed farming, which was Johnny's dream, but Jim said he was more interested in heading west. This suited Jason just fine; he knew there were mountains to the west, and he did so miss his mountains.

CHAPTER TWENTY-FIVE

Carey and Daniel

It was the summer of 1867. Carey, Daniel, and Em were wading in the creek below the cabin. Carey watched. Em was hanging on Daniel's arm, making monkey faces and screaming with glee every time he dipped her feet in the cold creek water. Her laughter was intoxicating, and Carey thanked the good Lord for letting her grow into such a happy child. Daniel couldn't have loved her more if she was his blood kin. She saved him from a life without a family, and Carey figured she had saved her from living without love after Jason had left. In these moments, Carey thought how ironic that such a sweet child could be the result of such a violent act; the war may have produced many such children as far as she knew. The stories the returning soldiers had shared were all frightening, especially the ones involving people's homes being invaded and even burned to the ground. Carey was grateful that her cabin and even her community had survived and were slowly returning to normal. Her little town had seen more than its share of wounded soldiers, both the maimed ones and the psychologically ruined ones, and of course, there were many who never returned to the mountains, assumed dead. Daniel had scars that he couldn't share with her and even now had dreams that he awoke from in fear and sometimes rage. Carey tried to get him to talk about the darker side of war, but he would only say it would be best if she didn't know the things he had done in battle. Occasionally he would get together with other veterans.

Carey assumed they would reminisce about the war, but women never attended these meetings. They always involved drinking, and Daniel would come home moody and depressed. After a while, Carey decided it was best if she didn't know the whole truth.

Looking around, Carey realized she was being left behind as Daniel and Em continued to splash and wade down the creek, jumping from rock to rock like wild Indians. They were almost to the falls when Em turned and yelled, "Hurry, Mama. We want to leap off together." Carey hated jumping into the cold water, but it had become a family tradition. Even in July, the chilly water would take her breath away and swimming to the nearby beach was laborious, but if Daniel could do it with only one arm and her five-year-old daughter thought it was a wonderful adventure for the family, then she was up for it. Em played quietly at the water's edge. Daniel and Carey lay on the sandy beach, letting the sun dry their clothes.

It had taken so long for the land and the people to return to normal. Carey felt relief. Taking the time for this family afternoon had made her think of her future and the little cove farm. Turning in Daniel's direction, she said, "Why don't we try raising some sheep?"

"What, now you want me to be a one-armed sheep herder?" came his response with a snicker that hurt her feelings.

"Why not?" she said.

"Let me think on it," Daniel said and fell in to a long silence. Carey knew him well enough to wait quietly while Daniel mulled it over. Several minutes later, Daniel told her all the reasons why sheep raising was a good idea and all the reasons it was a bad idea. He finished by saying Em would love every lamb, and selling them would be the only way to make a profit because he would not butcher them on the farm. Carey knew that Em would have handled the butchering idea better than Daniel, but she didn't mention that; instead she said, "What if we raise them for the wool, then we could shear them instead of selling or butchering?"

Daniel laughed and said, "You are always steps ahead of me." Carey and Daniel gathered up Em and headed for home by way of the wooded trail.

HOME

Em looked up at first one parent and then the other and said, "What's a sheep?"

Daniel scooped her up into his arm and said, "You'll find out purty quick, little miss." Two days later, Daniel returned from town with five lambs huddled on straw in the wagon bed. Em rushed out to see what a sheep was. Her excitement was contagious; Carey joined them. Daniel had lifted Em onto the wagon wheel so she could see, but before he could stop her, she climbed in and plopped down by the closest lamb, which she called Sam.

Turning in their directions, Em said, "This is Sam, the fat one is Chubby, the one with the spot will be Julia, that really fluffy one is Katie, and the black one . . ." She hesitated. "He's special. Let's call him Over!"

Daniel and Carey looked puzzled.

Daniel said, "Why Over, Emmie?"

"The war, it's over! That's a special thing, right?"

"I can't argue with that," Daniel answered. "Over it is!"

Carey said, "Okay, since that's settled, let's get them into the barn before it gets dark and every bobcat in the area gets a whiff."

Carey and Daniel carried the lambs two at a time into the barn, with Em supervising their movements closely. With Daniel's help, Em placed the water pails in the boarded stall and stood back to admire her sheep.

"Are they sheep or lambs?" Em asked.

When Daniel explained that they were baby sheep not yet fully grown, she understood immediately.

"Like me," she said.

Daniel agreed, "Yes, like you." He scooped Em up, Carey grabbed the back of Daniel's belt, and the family headed up the short hill to the comfort of the cabin. Carey looked at the original part of the cabin and had a fleeting thought of Jason. All the additions were Daniel's one-armed workmanship, but there was very little difference in the craftsmanship. Both men had been taught to work wood by her own grandfather when they were boys. The cabin had grown when Em was born, and then a rambling porch had been added to all four sides, which made it quite the mansion. The one-room cabin now had two bedrooms that were almost as big as the original room. The additions and changes had taken away the memories attached to the one-room cabin, both the good ones and the bad ones. Carey no longer thought of Jason when she entered the door and was indeed proud of all of it.

The sheep-raising idea had been something Grandmother had suggested. Carey missed her so. Carey tried not to remember her passing too often, but her dying words still haunted her. Grandmother had looked up at Carey and, with her dying breath, said, "He will be back!"

Everyone in the room said, "Praise Jesus," but Carey knew Grandmother spoke of Jason. She refused to let it disrupt her life with Em and Daniel, but recently Carey had been dreaming of a man on a pilgrimage, but his face was never revealed. Daniel had nudged her awake a couple of times. He never said, but she had the feeling she may have called out to the man in the dream. She thought it could be Jason.

Daniel was busying himself with repairing the fence lines. Carey put Em down for a nap and walked Daniel's lunch up to him. They sat under the poplar tree at the top of the cleared field and ate silently.

"Carey, I think all the bad that happened in the war is catching up to me."

Inwardly Carey was relieved; she had been worried that Daniel's silence had been about the dreams. However, she was definitely not ready for what came next.

"Carey, I'm ill. I rode down to town yesterday and talked with Doc. I have a disease and it is killing me. He gave me something for the pain, but I don't feel right taking it without telling you."

Carey felt like she had been punched in the stomach. Yesterday all was right with the world, and at that moment, the darkness closed in around her.

"That can't be right. You look great. When did this start? How long have you been hiding it from me?" Carey's mind was racing out of control, and her anger was building. "Why now? Just when things were finally looking good." Daniel reached out to her. She shook him off, jumped up, and ran back toward the cabin.

"Carey, wait," Daniel called after her. Daniel wished he had not told her. The last thing he wanted to deal with would be Em and Carey being sad. He went back to work on the fence, hoping that by dinnertime, Carey would be calm enough to talk. He remembered the last time he had seen Carey run away in anger all those years ago when he tried to take Jason to the war rally. I guess, in a way, fighting an illness was still a fight she didn't want to deal with. He would need to make things easy for them when he was gone.

Carey climbed over the pasture fence, and without realizing where she was going, she found herself at the tree with her and Jason's initials. She leaned against it and thought how she could not bear losing another man. Daniel had saved her just like Grandmother had said he would. Why would he be taken from her? Her anger grew. At first she was angry with Daniel then at Grandmother and finally with God. She let herself fall prey to the depression and loss, but then it came to her she could heal Daniel; Grandmother would have known how. All she had to do was study the old healing books that Grandmother had left for her when she died. Carey had stored them away; at the time, she was too busy with her own life to continue her education in the art of healing.

Each night when Daniel came in from the fence lines, Carey would be poring over Grandmother's remedies, searching for what would save him, but he knew it was no use. He had waited too long. He thought he should stop her and explain the situation, but he knew as long as she had a purpose, she would not interfere with his goal, which was to prepare the farm for his absence. He formulated the best way to go, but he would work until he could not, and then he would find a way to end the pain.

The more studying and reading Carey did into Grandmother's journals and remedy books, the more frustrated with Daniel she became; he had waited too late for this help. Carey had been to town and talked with Doc; he had explained what Daniel had not. The illness had progressed slowly in the beginning, and maybe the mountain remedies could have helped, but now it was just a matter of living out his life. The doc also told Carey other things that Daniel had failed to mention. Doc had served in Daniel's regiment and knew about all of his war injuries. He explained to Carey about the head injury that would always affect Daniel's thinking. Carey realized he was talking about the slower thought processing that she had only recently noticed. Daniel had always been a little slow, but she had not thought of it as a result of his war wounds.

"Carey," Doc said with gravity, "you must understand how damaged Daniel was by all of this! People only see the missing arm. In reality its loss is the least of his wounds. Even the procedure that took his arm has left him scarred beyond repair. It is hugely traumatic, and it occurred in the worst of conditions."

"I would like to be understanding, but he lied to me!"

"No, Carey, he believes he is protecting you and Em."

"But he has left me no way to help," Carey added with less anger.

"You must convince him to stay and let you care for him until the end."

"Stay?"

"Yes, he told me he is leaving so you will not need to care for him and Em will not see him die helpless."

"What would make him think that way? Daniel is the reason I survived at all."

"Everyone here sees that but not Daniel! You must convince him."

Carey walked home slowly. She tried to sort out all of what she had been told. She searched inside her own feelings and was saddened by the fact that occasionally the leaving thing seemed the best solution. She didn't want to deal with any of this; there was already so much to do. The sheep herd had grown, and winter meant so much work. If Daniel was unable to work, it would be too much for her. Em wasn't old enough to be of much help. They would have to hire someone. Then she would shake her head and think this was the wrong thought pattern.

Daniel could be around a lot longer. Doc had no time frame; they would fight this thing. If he kept himself strong, he could keep working, and right now, he seemed to be fine. She would find a remedy for strength and good health. She knew Daniel would follow her guidelines even if he thought it would do no good. She could convince him, then he would not follow through with his leaving plans. Doc told her that telling him she knew his plan for leaving would not help the situation. She would need to be smart. With her plan in place, she headed home after a quick stop at the "waiting spot" to survey the home front.

Daniel continued to work feverishly on the fence lines; they would all need to be completed before the spring lambs came. After his first lamb purchase, their herd had grown when an additional twelve sheep, most of them carrying lambs, came available. The price had been too good to pass on; besides, the purchase helped some neighbors who had fallen on some bad times. Daniel was all for expanding the sheep business, but when he looked at the endless rails laid out ahead of him, he felt overwhelmed. He thought if he would have all winter to build the fence, he could slow down, but his plans involved the winter months. No, the fences had to be ready by December, January at the latest, depending on the weather. When the spring lambing started, he would not be around to see it, but he knew they would be safe, and Carey and Em would have a cash crop for the farm.

Each night, when Daniel came in, dinner would be on the table, but before he could eat, Carey made him down a horrible-tasting drink that looked like green syrup. He drank it without knowing what it was in spite of the taste because Carey asked. He would do anything she asked. After about three days, he did feel he had more energy, but he knew it was not healing him as the pain also grew worse daily. He mostly ignored it; after the pain he had endured during the war, a gut pain wasn't that bad. He had only used the painkiller Doc had given him once because he believed it made him drowsy and worked against Carey's energy drinks. He needed to keep his thinking as clear as possible considering his plan.

CHAPTER TWENTY-SIX

Riverboat

Just as Jacque had described, the river was slowing down as they approached the last turn before the fuel landing. The curve caused a backflow, and this current slowed the boat, but Jacque also said that just around the bend and just ahead of the deer clearing, the current would pick up, sending the boat ahead at a quicker pace. Jason wasn't sure if it would come at a place during the aiming process or, when he was preparing to pull the trigger, it would depend on the deer. If they moved before the increase occurred, he might not have the lead time he needed on the buck. If the buck didn't come through, he would need to readjust and take a doe. He would trust in his visions and wait for the buck.

He did know, at an approximate distance of one hundred yards, the bell would sound the landing strike at which point the deer usually began to move according to Jacque. Jason would need to pick his back target before the bell sounded while watching the path the deer were taking. Jacque had said they normally ran parallel to the river about fifty feet off shore and then turned in away from the landing area. He thought Jason would have about twenty-five does to choose from and the big buck if he appeared.

The *Ohio Patriot* would be moving toward the shoreline while still steaming down the river with the flow. So many variables, but Jason had planned for all and could still see it working out in his favor. The shot itself would only be about half the distances of his earlier mission shots, but a moving target from a moving stand was all new to him. Jason felt nervous, not something that had accompanied all the other hard shots he had made. He welcomed the feeling of what the old-timers called "deer fever" even though it could affect his shot.

He felt the boat increase under his feet; he braced against the rail and raised the rifle to his shoulder. He could see the deer herd grazing quietly; when the bell sounded, all their heads came up in unison, and without a moment's hesitation, they began to move forward. Strangely, they did not run in panic; they just started to saunter off in twos and threes. As the boat pushed in closer to the shore, they began to run. Jason had a thought to just take a doe, but then there he was, the most magnificent buck he had ever encountered. He stood like a statue just inside the tree line. Jason's arm was fatiguing from holding the rifle with no brace, and his hands began to sweat. Neither phenomenon had been part of his previous experiences. In that second of self-doubt, the big buck stepped into view. Jason heard Jim and Jacque both inhale simultaneously; the rifle cracked in their ears. The buck leapt forward and, two strides later, crumbled to the ground. The crew cheered, even the ones who had bet against the shot meeting its mark.

Jason lowered the rifle, shook out his shoulder, and turned and saw Jim's smile. Jim laughed and said, "Reload. Shoot another couple! They're just hanging about."

"Sorry, no, one shot is all that is needed. My rifle and I have begun a new career."

When the boat was tied up, with the captain's permission, Jim, Jacque, and Jason made their way to where the buck lay. Captain Humphreys had requested the rack even before the betting started; had Jason had a place of his own, he might not have given it up. The buck was a twelve pointer, probably weighed in at 250 pounds.

"They grow big deer in Ohio," Jacque said.

"Biggest deer I ever seen," exclaimed Jim. "Oh my god, what a great shot! Jason Emerson will be known all along the Ohio River as the best sharpshooter east of the Mississippi."

Jason thought about that for a few minutes and then replied, "Then we may have to do some shooting when we get west of the Mississippi just to keep my reputation updated."

The three men smiled and companionably took on the task of butchering and preparing this massive deer for dinner and then some. Jason supervised instructing the city boy, Jim, how deer was used in his mountains, where nothing went to waste. Jacque was also interested in this job. He asked for certain cuts that he would use for his French recipes for the captain. Jason felt a great satisfaction in his skill and in his contribution to what would be the final dinner on this voyage. Cincinnati was the next stop for the *Ohio Patriot*, and the final dinner would be served on board during the last few hours before the landing.

Captain Humphreys invited Jim and Jason to the captain's table for the venison dinner prepared by Jacque. Most of the dinner conversation centered around the phenomenal shot that Jason had made from the *Ohio Patriot*. The captain's guests listened with interest to Jim's war stories and how he met Jason. When the conversation lulled, the older of the two men cleared his throat and said, "I have heard enough. They're hired."

Jason stood up abruptly and, looking around the table, trying to keep his voice controlled, said, "What is this, a job interview? This is how I ended up in Washington."

"Hold on a minute, Jason," Captain Humphreys announced. "It was not a setup. These fellows considering you for their job is a part of my winnings. I asked them here to meet you because they were looking for someone like you headed west with certain skills."

"Certain skills, like sharpshooting, an assassin, a murderer? I'm done with all that. Today was the first good shot I have taken since before the war. I'm done."

"Frankly, I wouldn't have introduced you if I thought that was your future. They need men with service experience to protect cargo through hostile country against wildcats and Indians. If you and Jim intend to see the Rockies, won't you need a job to get there?"

Jason felt embarrassed by his outburst. In retrospect, he knew Captain Humphreys wouldn't have set him up after the conversation they had the day the deer mission was established. The expression on Jim's face told Jason what a tragedy it would be if he let his guilt over the past and his emotions kill both their dreams. When they landed in Cincinnati, they would need some income above what they had won betting to start them on their way west.

The Overland Freight Company was well established. They had started hauling freight to the early gold areas around Denver even before the war had started.

Jason turned to the two men and said, "Who will decide who I fire on?"

The men exchanged looks, and the older man said with conviction, "You will decide. If your decisions are based on an eminent threat, the Overland Company will back you up. We expect you to defend the cargo and our drivers from the hostiles."

"Does that include murdering Indians?"

"We do not wish any harm to the Indians unless they are a threat. My company considers crossing their lands to be a necessary intrusion. Most of them have accepted us, but some, like the Pawnee, do not share those feelings."

"Well, I guess you have hired yourselves a security detail. Jim and I can start whenever we are needed."

"Good. We will have a load ready to leave within a couple of weeks of our landing tomorrow."

Jim walked around the table and slapped Jason on the back. The excitement showed in his face; he obviously was looking forward to his western adventure. Jason shook Mr. Thayer's hand, promising not to let him down. The Overland men watched them leave the dining room with some interest.

Mr. Thayer turned to Captain Humphrey and said, "He's a little volatile. Do you think he is going to be able to hold it together?"

"He has come a long way back from the brink of disaster. I believe he is more stable and still maintains some moral integrity, more than any of the others with his background, and he is definitely the best shot."

The second Overland gentleman added, "I'd be more concerned with Jim than Jason."

The three settled back at the table and sipped their brandy in silence.

CHAPTER TWENTY-SEVEN

Daniel

The time had come; the farm was prepared for the winter season, the sheep had substantial pasture, and Carey was distracted with plans for Em's birthday. He only had to wait for the first real freeze for his plan to be acted upon. His pain had gotten worse every day, and the doctor in town had insisted that he start taking the painkillers regularly. He found that the pain had started to make it hard to think clearly, but he was still intent on keeping Carey and Em from seeing his death. He would not be helpless in front of them. Ironically, Carey's remedies had kept him sufficiently energetic enough to continue to prepare to leave. He had thought it through; against Carey's constant nagging, he had left half the herd above the dark forest line. With the first sign of blizzard, he would have an excuse to go up to the mountain pastures. He would let the dogs push the sheep home, ride Aslan as far as he could safely take him, send him home, and do like the old Cherokees walk until he would succumb to the cold.

Carey came in from the barn; from the porch, she looked at the sky. She was immediately irritated; obviously, snow was coming, and Daniel had still not made time to bring the herd down from mountain pasture. Em's birthday was approaching; the herd had never been left this late. What was Daniel's problem? Was his mind going?

She stepped into the house and found Daniel lounging in front of the fire.

"Tomorrow you will go bring the sheep down!" she shouted at him.

"Actually, I was just thinking about that," Daniel said with a grin. "I'll go up first thing tomorrow."

Carey thought, *Finally*, not knowing she had played right into his hand.

Carey packed a lunch for Daniel and a potion and sent him off on Aslan in the early morning. He had looked in on a sleeping Em. He stood on the porch for a long time, staring at the mountain, and then hugged Carey, mounted, and rode away without looking back. Carey had watched him until he passed through the spot on the mountain where the trail turned upward and then gone back to her morning routine. She did not know that she had seen him for the last time.

The snow had already begun falling on the mountain before Daniel reached the herd, but he couldn't push them down until he knew Carey could not attempt to follow him. The timing would have to be just right. He needed the dogs to drive them home without his help, but they couldn't arrive until the blizzard hit the cove. By the time Carey would come looking for him, he needed his tracks to be covered; hopefully, his body would never be found.

When Carey and Em came in from the barn, the snow was falling. The storm came up very quickly. Carey was concerned about Daniel.

"Where's Daddy?" Em said.

"He's bringing the flock down from the mountain pasture."

"In the storm?"

"Yes, honey."

"Why did he wait so late? Will he be back for my birthday?"

"Of course," Carey said a little too quickly.

"It looks cold up there," Em said, looking up at the mountain.

"Just listen for the dogs. They'll be here by nightfall," Carey said reassuringly.

On the mountain, Daniel had gathered the flock and, with the dogs' help, was pushing them down the mountain road. Aslan acted confused when Daniel turned his head up the path and trotted away from the herd. He actually tried to turn back several times before letting Daniel direct him upward. Daniel's plan was proceeding as he had hoped. After about an hour of going up, the trail was not much more than a deer track and was disappearing under the falling snow. Aslan picked his way carefully along the rocky trail, cautiously testing the snow. Finally, as the storm intensified and Daniel could feel the temperature dropping, he dismounted. He adjusted the winter rug over Aslan's rump and turned him toward home. Before he sent him down, Daniel thanked Aslan for bringing him and Carey together. Remembering how they had met, he cut off the bridle reins to assure there would be no chance that Aslan would become tangled in the trees and not make it home. If Carey noticed this, his premeditation might be figured out, but by then, nothing could be done. Aslan trotted off toward the farm without hesitation. Daniel turned his back and walked farther into the dark forest. He found a tree big enough to rest his back against well off the trail, emptied the bottle of painkiller down his throat, and went to sleep. He left no note or apology; what he did was to save himself from watching his family watch him die. His last conscious thought was of Carey, Em, and his dear friend Jason.

The storm was relentless; the wind howled around the cabin. Em complained that she would not be able to hear the dogs or the sheep in time to greet them. Finally, as the light faded away, Carey convinced Em that it was time for bed. She could talk to Daddy in the morning. Carey knew she was lying. Daniel would by now be trapped on the mountain, and if the temperature kept dropping, he could be in real trouble. She could only pray that he had taken refuge in one of the old cabins near the high meadow.

"I hear the dogs," exclaimed Em from her room that was situated on the front of the house.

"Stay in that warm bed," Carey called back. "I'll go down and open the barn."

As Carey rushed down the path, she could hear the sheep as they shuffled through the snow and then their hooves on the bridge. The dogs had them bunched up tight and were working at the stragglers. She called orders to the dogs and watched through the falling snow as they filed into the barn. She busied herself counting, as was her habit, realizing that maybe five or six were missing. She closed the double doors and stared into the white snow for a sign of Daniel. Carey's insides began to churn; her earlier anger with him for waiting to bring them down so late rushed into her mind. Why would he have sent the flock down without coming with them? He must be gathering the lost ones, surely not in the storm, she thought. Where was he? Aslan would bring him home even if he was injured.

Carey found her way back to the cabin, only to find Em standing in the door. She was shivering from the cold and watching the mountain covered in snow with more coming down every minute. Carey bundled her up and carried her to the rocker in front of the big fireplace.

"We'll just wait here for Daddy," she said, trying not to sound worried for Em's sake.

Em whispered, "It's too cold on the mountain tonight! What if Daddy freezes?"

"Let's pray for him, Em. The good Lord will take care of him," Carey answered, knowing it was indeed in God's hands. They fell asleep in front of the fire. Carey dreamed of Daniel and Jason together, which was disturbing, but in the dream, it was Jason who walked toward home, not Daniel.

CHAPTER TWENTY-EIGHT

Jim and Jason

After landing at Cincinnati, Jim and Jason reported to the Overland Freight Company offices. They would be escorting a load of machinery to St. Louis, Jim's hometown, in a few days. Jason noticed that Jim could hardly contain his excitement on going home. They spent the next two days exploring Cincinnati. Jason actually enjoyed being a civilian for the first time since leaving Washington. Jim knew just enough about Cincinnati to keep them out of trouble.

Two days later, the freight wagons were ready. Jason was impressed. The wagons were pulled by oxen, teams of eight to ten oxen, some even matched. The drivers were a colorful bunch of tough men ready for anything but very appreciative to know they had an armed escort. Luckily, they all agreed that the route from Cincinnati to St. Louis would not require any protection—no hostiles, just an easy cross country drive to St Louis.

"You can always take the train. It is faster and most likely more comfortable."

"How long do we lay over in St. Louis?' Jim said.

The driver responded, "Oh sure, we'll stop off in St. Louis but not for long. From there to Westport, things can start to get dicey."

Jason liked the idea that he and Jim would have three hundred miles to learn how these people operated. Jason was glad to find out that the freight lines ran like a well-oiled machine. The drivers were definitely a capable bunch, and the herders kept the stock moving along agreeably. The overnight stops were either near a town or stations established by the freight company. The road was easily followed and well maintained. It followed almost the same track as the Ohio Mississippi Railroad.

The first time that he crossed over the Ohio and Mississippi Rail Road, Jim said with a touch of sadness, "Those are the tracks that took John and I to the war. It sure seems like a long time ago."

As a train rushed by and the drivers worked at keeping the teams from bolting, Jason could see the men in tattered uniforms crammed into open boxcars. The war had been over for almost a year, and these poor souls were just returning home. He had to consider himself lucky for the first time since he had left the mountains of West Virginia.

One of the drivers was a half-breed; his Indian name was Stands Alone roughly translated, but most of the men called him Red. Apparently, his mother had been taken in by one of the drivers. He was a noble-looking man, very tall; his facial features and his hair color were definitely Indian. Jason thought he seemed aloof.

The Indian approached Jason after hearing the story of his shooting off the riverboat deck.

"You are the sharpshooter, yes?"

"I would prefer if I were referred to as a hunter with an accurate aim. Why do you ask?"

"If you are to protect the drivers and the oxen and, of course, the freight, I would like to believe you are very accurate. There will be times when we get into Indian territory where a very long shot could stop an eminent attack."

Jason didn't like this man suggesting he shoot before they were attacked. It sounded like a sniper job, but he restrained from being too quick to judge.

"Why would you want your kin shot at without provocation?" he asked.

"You misunderstand," he spoke with haste. "My brothers will not attack if they know such a shooter is on the train. Even the fierce Pawnee do not wish to die for a few oxen. They will trade instead."

"If what you say is true, it could be a good piece of information."

"I offer it only because I have heard that you are not a believer in 'The only good Indian is a dead Indian.' It could save lives."

Then he turned and walked away. Jason watched him, wondering how he had ended up as a driver for the Overland Freight Company. He decided to ask another driver at the first opportunity. He wanted to know if this man could be trusted, not because he was an Indian but because of his attitude. The driver assured Jason that what he had been told would work.

"Yeah, the same ones that would attack a train will trade with it if it appears strong. They usually avoid the freight trains because of our numbers, but they can cause a lot of havoc by stampeding the oxen herds. If Red spreads the word about a sharpshooter, it will be safer for us."

"Spread the word? How would he do that?"

"He may be a white man's son, but he is still real close with his mother's people."

"Will I meet his father?" Jason asked.

"You met him. He hired you."

Jason considered this exchange carefully. An Indian and the boss's son, and he thought his life was complicated.

The closer they came to St. Louis, the more Jim talked about staying in the city. Jason listened to his talk about how easy life would be there, and he could find a wife and so forth, but he only became stronger in his resolve to go west. Whether Jim decided to stay was of no real importance to him or his plans. The mention of a wife did cause a different stir. He had never told Jim that he was already married—in fact still married but apparently replaced. He felt none of the ill will toward Carey that had come forward when he had last seen her. It had been so long ago, even the tragedies of the war didn't affect him like before. He guessed that time did heal wounds. He was able to put the war behind him, but Carey was a different matter altogether. She had been a part of him since their youth; no matter how he pushed her out of his head, thoughts of her and their home would interrupt him daily.

Jason tried to think of the opportunities ahead of him and block all the past out of his existence. The drivers began to talk about

Kansas and the great, monotonous plains. Some of them had been driving this route since before the war. They talked of the pioneers who trudged across the plains with handcarts loaded down with all their belongings, how on some days, hundreds of wagons would pass by; some were on their way to California. Jason wondered what would drive a man to uproot his entire family from their homes and march them hundreds of miles to an unknown destination.

The drivers would stare back at him and say, "Why are you here? What do you leave behind? Most who came before the war just wanted land of their own. Since the war, they run away from the tragedies of the war."

Jason thought about these statements for several days. The drivers came to make a living but always went back home after a run. Most of them had families in Cincinnati or St. Louis. It was at this point halfway to St. Louis that Jason realized he was running too, or maybe he was retreating. He was separating himself from the pain and death of the war and the loss of Carey. If he had thought going home and confronting Daniel and Carey could have worked out for anyone, including the unborn child, he would still have run the other way. After all the killings, his soul did not deserve even a chance at the happiness being with Carey would bring him. It was black and corrupted. Even if he had gotten control of the rage, he was definitely damaged goods.

CHAPTER TWENTY-NINE

Daniel

Carey awakened with a start; Em stood in the open cabin door in her bare feet. The wind was blowing her hair back into her face, and she had dropped the blanket that she had been wrapped in.

"Em," Carey started to chastise her for standing in the open door when she saw Aslan standing at the steps, alone. "Daniel!" she shouted.

"He's not here," Em whimpered. "There are no footprints. Mommy?"

"Come inside, Em," Carey said quietly and as calmly as she could. "You keep warm. I'll find him."

Carey knew Em's observation about the tracks told the whole story. Aslan had come back alone; Daniel was stranded, most likely dead on the mountain. All she could do would be to leave Em with someone and then go look. The storm had played itself out during the night, leaving the trees and the tracks covered in a foot of snow. It would have been a beautiful sight if not for the circumstances.

She replaced the broken reins on Aslan's bridle with a piece of rope, bundled Em up, rode to the nearest neighbor, the Baxters, and explained her situation. Em was not happy about being left behind but, as was her nature, did not cry. Carey hugged her and left without words. Em walked inside with the Baxters, an elderly couple who had been like grandparents to her. She sat down in front of the fire and began to entertain herself with a wooden horse that Daniel had made for her the summer before. She remembered how he had steadied the block of wood on his leather bench and, with his one hand, carved the magnificent replica of Aslan. He had told her how Mommy and Daddy had saved Aslan from his injuries and brought him home to the cove.

Em looked up at the old couple and said, "You know, Daddy is dead, but it's okay. He wanted to go."

The old couple looked at each other but did not respond; everyone suspected that this child had always been a seer like her great-grandmother. They didn't know what to say.

CHAPTER THIRTY

Carey

Carey pushed Aslan hard as they climbed the steep incline to the trail that overlooked the cabin. She had loaded enough warm blankets for wrapping Daniel for the trip home. Among these blankets was the bearskin that Jason had left with her in the last days before he left for the war. It would be the best way to cover the drag to bring Daniel down the mountain, assuming he was injured. She hoped in her heart that she would find him at the Cherokee cabins on the ridge near the mountain pasture, sitting against a wall in front of a roaring fire. Even injured, he could have gotten to shelter and survived the night.

The snow made the climb even harder; several times she was forced to find another way because of the deep drifts. What should have taken a couple of hours was already close to three hours. She knew another night on the mountain would be too much to endure. Ahead of her, she saw the mountain meadow; it was about four acres and looked like a white lake. The wind had been strong enough to push it into frozen waves. Carey started across to where she knew the cabins were, but there was no sign of smoke at the chimney. She kicked Aslan into a climbing canter; he jumped across the frozen snow, sometimes sinking to his knees.

"Stop," she said out loud, reminding herself how much the horse had already given her. Aslan stopped abruptly; she guessed he must have thought she was yelling at him. Then instead of going to the nearest cabin, he turned up the trail toward the upper pastures. Carey pulled on the reins, but he kept going and quickened his pace. Aslan continued up the mountain, following the trail that he had come down the night before. After about a mile, he lowered his head and stopped at the base of a large tree. Carey realized what she saw was not a snow drift against the tree; it had a recognizable shape, and she began to cry.

She also knew that this was no accident. Daniel had chosen this death. She thought she had convinced him to stay with her and Em as long as he could, let them care for him, and be with him until the end. When she let herself think back over the last two months and even yesterday morning, she realized he had been planning this. The war had caused this; fighting and being around death made men unable to accept any self-weaknesses. If Grandmother had not sent Daniel to help her, he probably would have succumbed to his depression and ended his life when he came home crippled. Carey dropped to her knees and let out a scream that caused the creatures in the woods to feel her pain at this loss.

This damn war still plagued the lives of good mountain folks even after it was over. Every family had lost someone or a part of someone to the brutality of a war that had changed very little in their existence. They hadn't owned slaves, they weren't part of the cotton industry, the railroads had not come to the mountains, and now Carey had lost another part of her heart. This was a good man; he would be missed.

Carey prepared the travois, using the bearskin as its base. Daniel's body was frozen, but she was able to position him on his side, and once the blankets were laid over him, he looked like he was sleeping peacefully. Carey kissed him on the forehead and wrapped the last blanket securely around his face, attached the side supports to the saddle, and started down the mountain. She would just make it home before dark.

As she walked, she cried. She cried for Daniel and all the boys who had come home wounded both in body and in mind and, of course, for the ones, like Jason, who were never seen again. She even thought about Em's biological father, who would never know his child, and how glad she was not to be alone. Her thoughts were interrupted by talking, and she looked for a place off the trail to hide. Fear was about to overwhelm her when she recognized the voice of one of Daniel's veteran friends.

"Carey, that you? Did you find him?" he shouted.

"Yes," she replied loud enough to be heard.

The men knew by the silence that followed that Daniel was dead.

As the small group of men appeared like a black smudge in the snow, Carey asked, "How did you know where we were?"

"I stopped in at the Baxters', checking on them after the storm. They said you had gone to look for Daniel near the mountain pasture. We saw the tracks."

"Did he fall from the horse? What happened?"

Carey, a little too quickly, said, "Yes, must have hit his head and froze."

The looked that passed between the men, all veterans with missing parts, told Carey what she suspected. They all knew the nature of Daniel's death. They had been on their way from town since morning, maybe hoping to stop him but more likely to help her bury him. They walked to the house with her, and while Carey went to fetch Em, they built a fire and burned a patch of ground so they could dig a grave. They had buried too many men since the war began and since it had ended.

CHAPTER THIRTY-ONE

Jim

Even though Jim had done nothing but talk about St. Louis, Jason was astonished at the size of this town. As the slow-moving oxen at the front of the freight train crossed over the railroad. Jason, who was on the sixth wagon, could see buildings taller than what he had seen in Washington; row after row, they seemed to continue endlessly.

"Isn't it great?" Jim exclaimed. "There's more than when we left."

Jason was, in fact, speechless. He just stared forward, trying to see how far the city extended. The freight train started to make a turn toward the freight yards located somewhere south on the riverfront; the landscape changed in that the buildings were smaller, but he still could not see the end of the street.

Jim was carrying on a conversation, but Jason only caught pieces. There was so much to see. As they traveled along, the buildings seemed to loom over him like a forest of trees but not near as comforting, and he felt like he had in Washington, trapped.

The drivers turned their teams into the big freight yard and stopped.

Jason looked at the driver whose wagon they were sitting on and said, "What now?"

"Simple, talk to the boss man in the office. Collect your pay. He'll tell you when to be back to leave for Westport."

Half an hour later, they were walking down the streets of St. Louis, the biggest town west of the Mississippi. Jason needed a drink. Jim conducted them to the places of his youth. In fact, they walked into the same bar that Jim and Johnny had had drinks the night before they took a train east to fight.

The barkeep took one look at the two filthy travelers, and Jason thought he was going to ask them to leave when a voice from the back shouted, "Is that you, Jim, my boy?" A mountain of a man strolled toward them with his arms stretched out wide. He clasped Jim in a big bear hug that left him trying to catch his breath.

When he could, he turned to Jason and said, "Meet my da', James McCrea."

"Da', this is Jason, my only living friend from the war."

Jason extended his hand but found himself suffocating in the same bear hug from Da' as Jim got.

Then he fairly shouted at the barkeep, "These boys deserve a drink. They are returning veterans of the worst war ever fought no matter which side you fought on."

Everyone in the bar shouted "Welcome home, lads!"

Jason didn't remember much of the rest of the night but awoke the next morning in a grand four-post bed. He could tell that he was in a hotel grander than anything he had ever seen. He drew back the window curtains and could finally see the edge of St. Louis as his room was on the top floor. It turned out that Jim's da' was the manager of the Lindell Hotel, which was in the process of being rebuilt, but instead of taking his drunken son and his drunken friend home to Momma, he put them up for the night at the Planter's Hotel.

Jason, James, and Jim walked to the McCrea home. James took them by the construction site of the Lindell and explained how close they were to reopening. Jason noticed that he mentioned something about jobs and how long was he staying. The way it came out, it sounded as if he had assumed Jim would be staying. Jason avoided the job-related questions. Jim didn't answer them either. Jason was already sure he would not be staying, but he would let Jim make his own decision. Family was a strong pull, and Jim had been gone for four years.

The thought of family and how long he had been gone brought Carey and Daniel to mind. Their kid would be three or four. It was difficult to remember the cove, his home; he had been gone for more than four years. With a little thought, he realized he had been gone for five years, three hundred sixty days, and about six hours. Jason reminded himself he had decided not to look back; his future lay to the west.

Jim's homecoming was quite the affair. During the night, James had spread the word about the return of his son. He had invited what appeared to be the entire neighborhood. Jim was overwhelmed but thrilled. Jason very quickly sought a place away from the crowd. Some folks approached and introduced themselves, but he wasn't much on long conversations with strangers.

Just when he thought he had found a good spot to observe without interaction, a young woman cornered him with her eyes. She was very attractive and maybe a little younger than he. When Jason saw that she had been seeking him out among the other guests, he stood when she arrived at his perch on the back-porch railing.

She extended her hand and introduced herself.

"My name is Alice. I know who you are, and I need to know, how did Johnny die?"

The question was blunt and came out quickly. It startled him, so without a thought, he answered defensively, "I wasn't there!"

Her tone softened, and she said, "Jim must have told you how it happened."

"Why don't you ask Jim?"

"He won't be able to tell me. We were all too close."

Jason remembered the stories from the cave about Alice. She was their girlfriend all through their youth. She was their first love. They had shared her affections right up to the day they had gone east to fight. She needed to know how Johnny had been killed, but Jason didn't think he could or should be the one to tell her.

Alice pleaded with him, but Jason could not bring himself to tell her. He simply suggested she give Jim time, and he was sure he would be able to fill her in.

Alice appeared confused; she looked into Jason's face and said, "But he will be leaving with you. I have no time."

"I think you will find Jim is very close to staying in St. Louis. He just needs a little encouragement. It's a fresh start. Help him find the way," Jason said softly. It felt like a betrayal, but Jim deserved the family he talked about before the war had consumed him.

Alice smiled, thanked Jason, and walked across the porch in the direction of Jim's voice.

The next morning, Jim told Jason he would be staying in St. Louis.

Jason laughed and said, "Alice didn't waste any time."

Jim acted surprised.

"She never was one for not following her heart. I'm not sure it would have worked this way if Johnny had made it home."

"I don't know if Johnny would have stayed in St. Louis long enough. He was bent on the westward movement. She seems happy here, and you can make her a good life with your da's help."

CHAPTER THIRTY-TWO

Carey and Em

After the burial, Carey held Em until she fell asleep. She was uncertain of how Daniel's death would affect them. The same fears and frustration rose in her from all those years ago, when she had been left alone in the cove. A woman alone in the hills with a small child would be difficult. She carried Em to her bed and covered her with Grandmother's quilt. As she stood up, she gently slapped her hands against her thighs and resolved to go on as before. Daniel had been preparing for the shearing all along. Their sheep operation could continue for the next few months without any additional help. By spring lambing, she would find some help.

Carey fell back into her own bed and was asleep almost immediately. About four o'clock in the morning, she reached across for Daniel's shoulder; when she remembered why he wasn't there, she cried. Then she dreamed of Jason. It made her feel guilty.

The dream took her back to their childhood, all the wonderful memories. In the memories, Daniel kept appearing and reappearing once before she and Jason had kissed. Then at Grandmother's house, the three of them having lunch, Grandmother looked so young, her smiling face so comforting. Just as she woke from her dream, Grandmother said, "Your lives will be forever entwined!" Carey had always thought that statement was directed at her and Jason, but in the dream, Daniel was included. She thought what it could mean now that their lives were completely separated. Daniel dead, Jason most likely dead as well, though she had never quite accepted that he was dead, only that he was gone.

She shook the thoughts away and started the morning chores; now was not the time to be looking back. She stoked the fire and warmed some water for Em. As she prepared the cabin for the day to come, she also formulated a plan. The farm's schedule would have to change; she would delegate some of the lighter chores to Em so that she could do what Daniel had been doing and what she had been doing as well. The process was very similar to five years ago, when Jason had left the farm.

Carey wasn't actually sure where to begin when she arrived in the barn. Daniel had left everything in order; even his small desk was cleared, except for a ledger. A great sadness crept over her as she sat down in the chair. Em was throwing feed for the chickens just outside the barn. She was singing. Her sweet voice drifted in and seemed to calm Carey. She slowly opened the ledger, and inside was a handwritten note from Daniel.

It said, "Carey, I am sorry that I was not strong enough to stay longer, but for me too early was easier than too late."

"Mommy," Em said tentatively; Carey hadn't heard Em come into the barn. She quickly wiped away her tears.

When she turned around, Em said, "I miss Daddy, but I'm not going to be sad. He wanted to go."

"I know," Carey answered. "I won't be sad either."

Carey and Em never cried over Daniel after that day. They told each other stories about him, things that he had done with each of them individually—life's adventures that the other one would not have known about. Carey was amazed at the lessons Em had learned from Daniel. The days became weeks, and the farm continued along smoothly. Carey spent evenings teaching Em to read and write.

CHAPTER THIRTY-THREE

Jim

Jim was able to procure a job in the freight offices, so even though he would not be heading west with Jason, they would still have a connection of sorts. Jason would join the security team again on the next leg of the journey west.

St. Louis to Westport was a distance of 238 miles; according to the drivers, it was normally fairly uneventful. The first leg of the trip, they traveled along the northern banks of the Missouri River. They turned onto the Boonslick Road, which most of the drivers call the Osage Trail. Jason questioned the others about the Indians; he was told most of them had moved west ahead of the settlers, and the ones who had stayed were mostly beggars and lived poorly. Jason had assumed that as a guard he would mostly be dealing with hostile Indians, but his first encounter was with a couple of veterans who tried to rob the food supplies.

The stop was at a well-established way station near Arrow Rock, about fifteen miles up the Missouri from Boonville. The Arrow Rock landing had become one of the busiest river ports due to all the travelers and the freight lines. Since it was already a regular stop, the drivers had secured their wagons and scattered into town for some entertainment, leaving Jason and a few others behind to keep the freight and supplies safe. On one of his walks around the wagons, Jason heard a commotion coming from near the food supply wagon. He went to investigate; as he got closer, he could hear voices.

"Take only what you need for now!"

"Grab a piece of bread for Josh."

"My, my, there's smoked meat in here."

The voices got louder as Jason got closer. In their excitement over finding food, they had forgotten where they were and what they were doing. Jason came around the back of the wagon with his gun lowered. He stood quietly and observed this ragtag group of young men, not much more than boys. They were dressed in the remnants of uniforms so tattered that Jason couldn't decide whether they were blue or gray, with no visible weapons among them. Jason had seen hungry soldiers, but this group looked like prison-camp survivors; they were skeletons just covered with skin and rags.

Jason cleared his throat and said, "You boys know that food is the property of the freight lines?"

The three men whirled as one to face him, all eyes on the rifle that Jason had trained on them. One of the men dropped to his knees and placed his hands on his head.

The man on his right reached down and said, "Get up, Jack. He is not going to shoot us."

The other man said, "Maybe that would be best. Starvin' in prison was understandable, but starvin' around so much food is downright tormentin'."

Jason lowered his rifle slightly. This boy's accent made him think of home; it definitely had a mountain tone.

"Where you boys from?"

"If you mean home, it's East Tennessee, but we are traveling east from Fort Leavenworth, Kansas. What do you plan on doing with us?"

"That depends on what you plan on doing with that food."

"I'd really like to eat it," the youngest boy said with hope in his voice.

The taller boy, who seemed to be in charge of the group, said, "Tell us what you think is fair, and please let us go back to our camp. There's another member of our squad who can't walk without us, and food or not, he will die without us."

Jason could see the concern in the boy's face, but before he could speak, Red walked into the light cast by the hanging lantern. He surveyed the situation and motioned for Jason to join him at the edge of light. When he was close enough, Red said, "Let them go with the food. We have plenty."

"Why would you do that?"

"They have suffered enough. They will need strength to make it home. Don't they deserve that much considering all they have obviously been through in the war?"

"Yes, I agree, but what about the company?"

"I guess I'm only half a company man. The Indian half has been taught a bigger picture. This kindness may give them the chance to go forward to something better."

Before Jason could respond, Red slipped away as quietly as he had appeared. Jason returned to the three frightened boys and said, "You heard the man. Take what you can carry, but don't try this again. There are white men on this duty that would just shoot you."

Jason watched them fill their bags, turned, and started his rounds again. They shouted thanks, and as they started away, the boy whose face had been somehow familiar to Jason said, "Thanks, Jason. Hope you find your way home to our mountains."

All three bolted into a run and were caught up in the shadows of the wagons piled high with freight. It didn't hit Jason until several hours later that the boy had called him by name. He didn't remember giving them his name; he most certainly had not, so how did the kid know it? And he said "our mountains"; that boy was from West Virginia. He regretted that he would not have time to search for their camp before his departure but was relieved at the same time since he knew news of home would include Carey and Daniel.

CHAPTER THIRTY-FOUR

Jason and Red

The rest of the journey to Westport was uneventful, just as the drivers had predicted. Jason was able to ride horseback for part of the journey and scout around the countryside with Red. The land was vast and so flat compared to his home. Red talked about the Rockies and told Jason that there was really no comparison between them and the Appalachians. Jason was sure the Rockies would be impressive but was also sure they would never take the place of the green mountains of his home.

When he could ride far enough to escape the endless stretches of wagon-trodden grass, the tall grasses waved in the wind and seemed to go on forever. There were two and sometimes three lines of travel a mile or two apart, all headed west. The track the wagons took depended on how wet or dry the areas were and whether the loads were light or heavy. If the crossing were closer to the head of a stream or river, the shallow waters made for less losses of livestock or humans; most travelers did not swim. The snake-infested Missouri had not been a place you wanted to take a swim or bathe in for that matter. Some of these smaller creeks were refreshing and clear like the mountain streams of his youth.

Westport was the jumping-off spot, the last real civilization. The town had become the exchange center between the river and the Santa Fe Trail. The westward bound would supply their wagons for the trip ahead at this point, buying enough provisions, in some cases, to travel all the way to California. After Westport supplies became scarce and far between. Jason thought it took great courage to plan a trip to California as a prospector, but taking a family was irresponsible at the least. He was glad that Jim had stayed in St. Louis with his new wife. He could travel to California when the railroad was complete.

During a stop at Willow springs, Jason got a chance to talk with Red. He was concerned about what to expect from the Indians and knew Red would be less biased or reactionary than the other drivers. He found Red sitting with a group of men; they were not freight-company employees. When Red saw him, he motioned for him to join them.

"I've just been discussing the trail ahead with these traders," Red said and then introduced Jason to the group.

Their forthright stares made him a bit uncomfortable.

The silence was broken when an older mountain of a man thrust out his hand and said, "The sharpshooter, I heard about you, hopin' we would meet. If I had shot a deer off the deck of a moving vessel, I would have had a dime novel written about it. How is it you have remained so uncelebrated?"

Jason couldn't find his voice quick enough to respond. Red was looking at him with surprise as well. Jason couldn't imagine how this backwoodsman could have heard about the deer. While he stood bewildered, the man told the story to the others—well, a somewhat-embellished version. He tried to interrupt, but they would have none of it.

Finally, Jason interjected, "It wasn't all that special."

The older man grabbed him by the shoulders and said, "Don't be so humble. This is a big country, so ordinary becomes extraordinary."

The discussion that followed was about the trail ahead. Red was inquiring of these men what the Indian situation was near Pawnee Rock and if any of the crossings were going to be more dangerous than usual. Jason had heard about Pawnee Rock or Rock Point. It was an observation point that jutted up 150 feet above the surrounding plains. A man standing on the top, looking out over the green below, could see the approach of anything from all directions.

Most of the nearby tribes still living on the plains of the Kansas territories honored the agreement made at Council Grove in 1861. At the time of the signing, it was the Osage who agreed to allow the settlers to pass through their territory. Other tribes who occupied the huge expanse of windswept prairie were not so accommodating. If they caught a small group of travelers in the open without the presence of a controlling military force, it could turn ugly. According to these men, things were heating up, and the raiding parties were definitely seen near Pawnee Rock.

When Red and Jason were alone, Red said, "We are still two hundred miles or so from Pawnee Rock, but it would be good to have a plan."

"What do you have in mind?" Jason queried.

"I'm thinking you and I could set up an observation point on Pawnee Rock ahead of the approach by our drivers. If you are as good a shot as I've been told, you could discourage any would-be attackers from a far."

Jason's guts churned. Was he to become an assassin again?

Then Red said, "Are you accurate enough to miss from the same distances as you have killed from in the past?"

Jason relaxed and pondered this question a moment.

"Yes!"

"Perfect. I will let the bosses know our plans, and we will leave for Pawnee Rock in a couple of days."

CHAPTER THIRTY-FIVE

Jason and Red

Jason and Red traveled on horseback, bringing with them one pack horse. They took turns leading the pack animal and traveled along a whole heap faster than the freight wagons. Red explained that the route they followed would bring them onto Rock Point from the north. It should draw less attention, and hopefully, they would be in place without any encounters with war parties.

Jason had wondered if Red had worked out a plan for avoiding any confrontations before they reached Pawnee Rock, but he was enjoying the fast pace and the countryside. They made a short stop at Council Grove then pushed on to Fort Zarah. They rode like pony express riders, reckless at times, but because they didn't have the luxury of extra horses, there were long stretches of walking.

During these slow times, Jason began to understand Red. He talked about his mother and his youth. He had virtually been raised on a freight wagon. His father had found his mother, an Osage woman, abandoned on the trail. She had been taken from her tribe as a young girl by the Pawnee and sold to a white trader. When she was found, she was already pregnant with Red. The man whom Red called father was not his blood, but Red had only recently learned of this. Jason could find no bitterness or depression in Red's voice. He simply accepted these things without concern.

"So how did your mother come to be abandoned?" Jason asked.

"That is something she has never discussed with me, but the traders say she killed the man she had been with," Red answered with a shrug. "She is strong," he added with a laugh.

"Some women have that kind of strength," Jason said and thought of Carey.

They had reached the Great Bend of the Arkansas River; instead of following the worn wagon tracks, Red took them straight out into the grasslands. Jason would have been concerned, but Red seemed to know the way. If you paid close attention to the grass patterns, there were game trails, and he spotted the occasional antelope in the distance. They traveled due north for a while and then made a slight westward turn, riding into one of the most beautiful sunsets Jason had ever witnessed.

They camped in the middle of a great expanse of grassland. Red asked Jason if he had spotted Pawnee Rock. Jason looked at the horizon, turning as it continued in a circle around him. No matter how hard he stared, he saw nothing but flatland and grass.

"In the morning, I will show you. We will rest here and approach just before dawn."

"Why at dawn?" Jason inquired.

"If anyone is on top with the sun in their eyes, we can approach undetected."

"Do you expect it to be occupied?"

"I hope by Osage friends, but we must be cagey. Get some rest."

Jason took one last look in the direction Red had indicated; he may have seen a difference in the color of the green. By the time he remembered his gun scope, the darkness had completely enveloped the campsite. Without trees, the darkness seemed thick and sinister. Jason felt way less safe than he had in his cave.

*****

What seemed like minutes had been hours of restless sleep when Red nudged him awake.

"Time to go," he whispered.

Jason leaped up, took the reins of his horse, and walked beside Red and his horse, pulling the pack horse along behind. They walked in silence; Jason wasn't sure why. He knew they had to be several miles from the rock outcropping. Red stopped. Jason stopped.

Red pointed out six horses approaching from the north. They were traveling fast. Jason readied his gun. Looking through the scope, he could see Indians. They rode with grace; they were like extensions of their ponies. He waited for Red to instruct him on whether they were in danger. As he watched, the Indians turned and rode west on a route that would take them away from the path he and Red were traveling.

Red put a hand on Jason's gun, and he lowered it.

"They are in quest of bigger game," he said. "Look ahead of them. That moving cloud of dust, buffalo, looks like a big herd. This makes our chances of keeping the rock to ourselves even better. Any tribe in this area will move on the herd, taking them farther north."

"If they hadn't seen the buffalo, do you think they would have attacked us without provocation?"

"Whites massacre Indians. Indians massacre Whites. Most men cannot remain calm when they find their homes destroyed and their families mutilated. The next man they see is fair game. Revenge is the face of this war of the plains."

CHAPTER THIRTY-SIX

Jason and Red

Red's assumption that the Indians would be occupied with the buffalo seemed to be the case. Their approach to Pawnee rock was just a quiet gallop across flat grasslands. About a mile out, what had appeared as a change in grass color the night before took shape, rising above the horizon. They were riding toward a cliff face covered with small shrubs. It rose above them; one hundred fifty feet, from a distance, the colors had blended into the green fields behind, making it camouflaged.

Red dismounted and said, "Tie the horses here. We'll come back for them."

He then skirted along the base of the cliff until he reached a trail. The climb was made easy by the carved-out rock steps. Along the rock wall, pioneers had carved initials and dates; some were as early as 1776.

Jason thought about the earlier explorers of this area before the settlers who traded with the Indians and made friendships; some even married into the tribes. These marriages made them a part of the community and eligible for all that the tribe could offer. The Indians believed in mutual benefit; the whole idea of selling things for income made no sense within their culture. The conflicts over land were beyond their understanding. No one owns the land. It must be protected from misuse by all, but no one owns it. The settlers wanted ownership, which was the complete opposite, and Jason understood how the Indians were confused.

Nearing the end of the climb, Red slowed his pace and made gestures indicating for Jason to be quiet. Jason complied and prepared for whatever the top might bring. With a quick movement, Red vaulted onto the flat top of the rock. Jason followed immediately behind, tensed and ready for some sort of encounter. Over time most of the area on the top had been cleared or trampled down by campsites and human occupation. One lone tree stood guard atop the rock, its roots planted deep in the rock's crevices. Jason and Red were the only inhabitants.

"Relax, and enjoy the view," Red said. "It looks like we have secured our vantage point without any killing."

Jason did relax, but he was realizing that he had left one war behind and traveled a long way to be involved in another. This war had no clear-cut objective either; it was a cultural clash as well, but the factions in this war did not come from a common background. The American settler had a unified army to back them, and the Indians were protecting their families from an enemy they did not understand. This was a hostile takeover of their land, which was changing the entire fabric of their lives.

After deciding what the most advantageous lookout site would be, Jason and Red descended the rock and retrieved their horses and supplies. Once their camp had been established, they took turns checking in all four directions for anyone approaching their secured location. Jason fell back into the detailed observation techniques he had learned during his sniper training.

No matter which direction he looked, the plains appeared never ending, but with closer study, he began to see distinctions. Looking east, Jason could make out the tracks left by all the wagons moving west over the past years. Looking north, he could just make out the swath of eaten grass left by the herd of buffalo they had seen earlier. To the south, the river was a winding ribbon of color; not quite blue, it disappeared in between the line of trees growing along its banks. Westward, Jason could once again pick up the wagon ruts left by the endless migration of settlers and freighters, some of which would be headed southwest at Fort Larned to Santa Fe. He knew that his train would take the mountain cutoff and be headed for Fort Bent, or what was left of Fort Bent after the Mexican–American War.

Red believed the freight wagons could be visible within three days' time, so he and Jason passed the time collecting water and wood for cooking. They talked mostly of what they planned to do if any hostiles approached the rock. Red said because of their advantage point, they could see all movements on the plains, and it would be easy to recognize a war party from a friendly group.

Early the next morning, Jason noticed movement on the trail; it was too soon to be the freighters, but it moved like wagons. As the little train approached, he counted fifteen wagons.

Red appeared at his shoulder and looked toward the wagons and then to their left. Jason followed his gaze with the scope and saw riders moving fast.

"Stop them, Jason!" Red calmly shouted.

"How do you know they are hostiles?"

"Easy, they are moving way too fast for travelers, traders, or trappers. That is a war party, I'll bet on it."

"You would bet their lives," asked Jason.

"No, I'm betting one well-executed miss will stop them. You are the guy who killed a running deer off a moving steamship, right?"

"Right," Jason said, lowering his rifle. He began to calculate the range to his target. He watched closely as the riders continued to angle toward the slow-moving wagons.

At the same time Jason squeezed off his first shot, the settlers had seen the approaching menace. They stopped the wagons and tried to prepare for the eminent attack as best they could.

The first shot landed in the dirt about ten feet from the lead pony; he spun and almost put his rider in the dirt. Jason could see the hesitation in all the ponies when the sound of the bullet reached them. His second shot hit the ground to their left, sending the shying ponies to the right and away from the direction of the wagons. Jason reloaded and waited to see what the group of Indians had decided.

Standing behind him, Red said, "The wagons are moving again."

HOME

Jason looked at the wagons and then quickly back at the war party. The plan had worked; they were angling northwest, away from the wagons and Pawnee Rock. Jason recalculated and sent one more shot in their directions; this time he thought he actually might have clipped the heel of the last pony in the group. It bolted forward, galloping through the others and taking over as lead pony.

"I knew this would save lives. That was amazing!" Red shouted, clapping Jason on the back. "Let's go greet those lucky travelers."

Jason opted to stay on the rock. He just wasn't ready to talk about his shooting. He would have to do a lot of saving lives to be cleansed of all the murders he had committed during the war. The sounds of conversation and celebration from below were enough of a thanks.

Jason was watching the sunset when he heard Red and two men clambering up the steep trail. Red introduced the two men, Jake and Frank, trail bosses, or guides, for the small train. Jake handed him a plate of food.

Frank waited until Jason had his mouth full and said, "Thanks for what you did. We would have simply perished at the hands of those Injuns."

"That's right. Even though every man has a gun, most of this group has never fired at another human being. Just farmers and their families," Jake added.

Jason could only nod since his mouth was full of the best food he had had since leaving Ohio. The two men talked on about the difficulties of the trail. Red suggested, with so few wagons, they might want to wait for the freight wagons before going on to Fort Larned. Jake said that had been their plan, but the freighters had been stopped by some axle issues, so they had pushed on. They had known about the Pawnee Rock observers from conversation with the freight drivers but hadn't supposed it would matter as much as it had.

"Yeah, your wagons were our test group. Glad my plan worked," Red said with a smile.

The two men stood, but before heading back down the incline, they both shook Jason's hand and thanked him again for saving their lives and the ten families bound for California. Red had cautioned them not to ask Jason about his skill with a gun. He also assured them that if they waited and traveled on with the freight wagons, Jason would have their backs as they headed out onto the open prairie ahead.

The wagon company decided to wait for the freighters as Red suggested, so for the next two days, food on the Rock continued to remind Jason of home. A different member of the traveling party would deliver him lunch and a dinner basket. Jason tried to be cordial, but he found it a distraction. He had worked out an observation routine that flowed fairly smoothly if not interrupted.

Fifteen-year-old, John Kimball begged his mother to climb the rock and take lunch to the sniper. His mother was busy and agreed but cautioned him not to ask too many questions. She watched him almost jog to the steep path, knowing the sniper was not going to be able to enjoy his lunch today.

John approached the lookout with more caution than he had used climbing the rock trail. The Indian was sitting to one side of the sniper. He watched John but did not speak. The sniper was sweeping the horizon with his rifle. He would scan then pause and then start again. When he lowered his weapon, John stepped forward, offering him the basket of food.

Jason took the basket, lowered it to the ground next to where he was crouched, and said, "Stay and have lunch," to the boy.

"Are you sure? Ma said not to bother you."

"You have arrived at the right time. Red is going to watch while I eat."

Red looked surprised but instantly agreed. Jason shared his food with John. John couldn't keep from staring at the rifle.

After a while, he mustered up the nerve to ask, "Tell me about the rifle."

Jason turned toward him with an expression that caused the boy to flinch. Realizing how he had reacted, he said, "Sorry, I don't really talk about the rifle."

The kid said, "Sorry, why not?"

And for no real reason, Jason began to talk about the rifle. He told John it had been a gift from his father. During the war, the gunsmith whose uncle had made the gun had removed all the beautiful silver. He explained that he needed to be less conspicuous to do his job. The more he talked, the easier it came out. He had replaced the silver on his way west because he and the rifle were putting the war and his soldiering behind them.

Red had taken over the watch, but he listened to this conversation; it told him way more about Jason's past than any conversation they had had on the trail before. John was fascinated by the entire discussion. His mother had said no questions; he had not needed to disobey. Jason had relayed a short history of his military career and his sniper training.

As abruptly as he had started talking, Jason stopped, picked up his rifle, and returned to his scanning. Red thanked John and sent him on his way. He wanted to pry into Jason even more but stopped when Jason said, "Look east!"

Red looked east; the first view of the freighters, a black smudge trailing out like a long snake, had appeared on the horizon. They were still a long way off and moving at the slow rate of the oxen. The protection detail was now at full attention.

Jason and Red hoped that word of the previous encounter had been spread enough to discourage any more attacks, but the freight train's livestock herds would be a great temptation. The long worm seemed to get ever longer, then the wagons separated onto two tracks forming two worms with the herds in between for protection from stampeding. It was quite the maneuver, but the drivers pulled it off brilliantly.

Now with the two lines of wagons about a mile apart, Red scanned to the south while Jason watched to the north. Red was worried that the attack would come from behind the cover of trees, and he knew if the braves were aware of Jason, they would wait until the route to the wagons was at its shortest. They would risk death for beef.

Jason observed some mule deer trotting lazily along about a half mile away. He thought they would be a good meal for someone but didn't dare shoot as it would reveal his location. In that moment, Red detected motion near the river; there were several horses moving slowly toward the camp wagons below. They were walking slowly with a pack animal covered with furs and other tradeable items.

"What do you think, Red, friend or foe?"

"I think friends. They look like Osage, but it could be a diversion. I'll go down and talk with them."

Jason continued to search the wide plains north and south for any activity out of the ordinary. He thought if it wasn't for this hilltop of rock, the vastness of these prairies would have sent him running for home. The boring grass waved at him, as if to say, "You don't belong here. Go away." The grass was like the Indians; it was not pleased with the destruction caused by the settlers. Jason saw no movement below, with the exception of the long row of wagons for as far as he could see. He supposed that this view was not much different from the view from the bow of a ship at sea, except the waves were greenish yellow instead of blue.

Red had been right; the Osage only wanted to trade. He had introduced them to the settlers, and Jake was helping them trade using sign language. By the time he returned to the rock, Jason was taking a break, leaning back.

"It seems the word has spread none of the people will risk the 'long rifle' according to the Osage, who did come in to trade. I think they weren't sure you wouldn't shoot them."

"How long will the freighters stay before moving on again?" Jason asked.

"Not long, they are behind schedule. We will cover them from here and catch up at Fort Larned."

"What's the Indian threat like the farther west we go?"

"If what the Osage told me is true, things are really heating up along the mountain cutoff, but we'll have a military escort with us then."

CHAPTER THIRTY-SEVEN

Amelia and Em

By the time the spring lambing began, Carey and Em had mostly adjusted to life without Daniel. Carey had hired a young girl from town to help with the herd. She had no family due to illness and, of course, the war, so she fit right in with all the survivors. Her name was Julia; she was always a bit melancholy. If she had wanted a man in her life, she would have had no problem. She was tall with long blond hair and blue eyes, but she told Carey she had had enough of men.

The maimed men who had helped with Daniel's burial pitched in with the lambing. Carey hoped it would bring them some joy, all the new life. She had been treating them with herbs and some other of Grandmother's medicine for their war injuries, both physical and mental, in return for their help. The more she knew of these men, the better understanding she had for Daniel. It had helped her forgive him for what he had done.

Her healing ways were fast becoming well-known in the local mountains. Many of the people remembered Grandmother and would come from quite a ways for Carey's treatment. Carey treated them all and would only barter in exchange. No money, service for service. Em always helped, and the women showered her with hand-made clothing. Carey was grateful since between the sheep and her patients, there was very little time for any sewing.

Meeting and greeting the new visitors became Em's main chore. Her small child's innocence broke down the suspicions of even the shyest of the mountain folk. It was especially helpful when an elderly lady appeared at the edge of the wooded lot. She had obviously come from deep in the hollows, traveling alone, and wanted Carey's assistance but would not approach the house.

"Can I go out to her?" Em asked her mother.

Carey answered, "No, let her be for now."

Em was concerned, but she simply did what she was told. After three days, the old woman had still not come forward.

So Em asked again, "Mother, can I go talk to the old lady?"

Carey heard the concern in the child's voice, and she had called her Mother instead of Ma, which she only used when things were important to her. Carey looked toward the camp and said, "Yes, but only go close enough to talk. Stay out of reach. She could be isolating herself for reasons other than shyness."

Em started in the direction of the woman's camp. She hesitated and turned back to Carey.

"Can I take her some cornbread?"

"Yes, she would probably like that, but remember not so close to be touched."

Em ran back to the cabin, folded some cornbread into a piece of cloth, and with a very determined gait, started across the pasture to the wooded lot. She stopped at the fence line and placed her little parcel on top of a corner post, thinking briefly about helping Daniel build the fence.

The old woman had stood and looked as if she were preparing to run into the woods. Em thought she looked very much like the young deer when they realized they had gone too far from their mothers. She had that same look of real instinctual fear. Em stopped all motion and slowly leaned against the top rail.

In her quietest, soothing voice, she spoke, "Good morning, the healer suggested I bring you some cornbread." Then she slowly turned to walk back the way she had come.

Before she had taken many steps, she heard the old woman say," Wait. Are you the healer's daughter?"

Em turned back in one very smooth motion, trying not to appear threatening. The old woman stepped back, but she didn't look as if she would bolt. She held the cornbread very protectively in her arms. She had more wrinkles than anyone Em had ever meet. Her shoulders were rounded to the point of there being the beginnings of a small hump at her upper back. The old woman was so short that Em thought she could be a dwarf.

"I'm not a witch," she said. "Don't run back to the house."

"There are no such things as witches!" Em said with a harsher tone than she intended.

The old woman flinched and said, "What makes you so sure?"

"My grandmother was not a witch either, but people said she was."

"Why, did they say she was a witch?" asked the old woman.

"Because she could see things that hadn't happened."

"Yes, I can do that as well."

"I dream things," said Em, "And then they happen."

"Did you dream about meeting me?"

"Why, no," Em responded. "Did you dream about me?"

"Come back tomorrow and we'll talk again." And she turned and walked away.

Em stood for a moment and watched the hesitant, rambling gait of the elderly woman. On her way back to the cabin, she pondered on their conversation. She needed to remember so she could tell her mother what had been said. She had not dreamed of this woman, but she seemed very familiar for some reason.

Em pushed the cabin door so hard in her haste that it flew back against the wall, making a loud noise.

Carey looked up and said, "Oh my, what is your rush? Was she that scary, perhaps a witch?" she added with a laugh.

Em laughed and said, "No, not a witch." This was their little private joke about the time when Carey was accused of being a witch anytime either of them did something disruptive or unexpected. "Oddly enough, that is what we talked about, witches."

"So she talked," Carey asked. "Did you find out what she wants?"

"Nope, we're going to talk again tomorrow. Maybe you should go with me. I think I may have seen her before."

"I can't see how. You have not been around any elderly woman since Grandmother passed. It's a mystery. Now, get ready for bed."

Carey watched Em go and thought, *What an amazing child. Even at six years old, she has an old soul.* Hopefully, the mystery of this old woman would be a good adventure for her child.

CHAPTER THIRTY-EIGHT

Amelia and Em

The old woman had watched the child skip away in the direction of the cabin, amazed that she was seeing her only living blood relative. The fact that her useless, no-good grandson had produced this exceptional child was a blessing for her old heart and a burden. She knew she could never tell her or her mother, the healer, of her connection to Em.

Carey continued to allow Em to venture out to the camp of the old lady. Each day she came back to the cabin with stories of kindness and empathy. Em told her mother about all their discoveries along the edge of the wood and their walking adventures. Carey reminded Em never to go out of earshot of the cabin and to be cautious with the elderly woman. Carey still didn't understand who she was or why she had showed up.

After two weeks, Carey decided it was time to walk out to the fence on her own to find out why. Em was busy helping with the lambs. When she reached the fence, the camp was abandoned. She called out, but no answer came. Carey knew it was an intrusive thing to do, but she climbed over and began to inspect the area that the old woman had made into a temporary home. Carey was amazed at how simply she was living. There were no personal items except for a few pieces of clothing and a tattered Bible. Carey bent down and picked up the Bible.

"Don't touch that," the old woman fairly shouted.

"Oh, I'm so sorry," Carey answered, startled by the sudden appearance.

Snatching the Bible away from Carey, she said with a meanness, "Don't you have any respect for others?"

Carey stared at the woman's eyes and saw something that worried her, a kind of recognition, but she knew they had never met before.

The old woman quickly softened her expression and said, "I'm sorry. I've been on my own for so long, I don't know how to behave. Please forgive me."

"No, I was out of line. I'm really sorry, but Em makes friends a little too easily."

The old woman smiled and said, "She is brilliant!"

Carey stepped back and studied the woman and immediately knew that no harm would come to her child from this.

"Please tell me what has brought you to our little cove."

"My name is Amelia. I have come a long way to get an herbal potion that I was told you have perfected."

"Why have you isolated yourself?"

"I needed to be sure I had the right healer, and then I met Em. I've really enjoyed sharing my mornings with her. And like I said, I'm used to being alone."

"You need to come have dinner with us," Carey said with a finality and then started back to the house.

Amelia watched her go. Dinner with her grandchild would be nice. Then she would take her potion and go back to her mountain home and die at peace, knowing she had at least a legacy. She would have to ask that her Bible be buried with her; it was the only record of Em's blood relationship to her.

The morning after the dinner with Amelia, Carey began to prepare the potion that she had requested. It was a complicated remedy, and it would take a few days to gather the needed herbs. Em and Carey packed a lunch and rode Aslan up into the higher elevations. Carey had not traveled up this high since Daniel's last ride, but the things she needed to collect didn't grow any lower.

When they reached the Cherokee cabins, they stopped for lunch. Em went to the spring to fetch some water. When she returned, Carey saw tears.

"What's wrong?"

"I couldn't help but think of Daddy. Aren't we near where he died?"

"Yes, very near, do you need to see where?"

Em shook her head yes and looked at her mother with a hopeful face.

"It's okay. Come with me."

Carey left Aslan grazing on the sweet mountain grass, took Em's hand in hers, and started up the trail above the cabins. Em remained silent until they reached the big oak. Carey stopped about ten feet away and stared at the base of the tree. Growing all around was the very plant she was searching.

"I saw this in my dream," Em said. "Daddy wanted us to come here today in my dream. Is this okay?"

"Of course, it's okay. Why do you ask?"

"Sometimes, it frightens me to know things before they happen."

"Understandable, but have you ever dreamed anything that caused you harm?"

"No, but I have dreamed harm that happened to other people."

"Em, I know a gift like yours can be frightening. Grandmother had to learn how to control it, how to tell what dreams were prophecies and what were just dreams brought on by living."

"How do I learn that?" Em asked very quietly.

"We will have to study on that, but not yet."

Em nodded in agreement with her mother. Carey tried not to show her concern; she really wasn't sure how she could help with this problem. Em may be an old soul, but she wanted to protect her for as long as she could from the trials of her grandmother. Carey had always felt lucky that this particular gift had skipped a generation.

Amelia was resting on the porch when they returned. Before Carey had finished unloading, Em was telling her all about their ride. She had climbed up into her lap, just as Carey would have with her grandmother. It made Carey smile. She gathered up her herbs and went inside to start the preparation of the potion.

Carey could hear bits of the conversation from the porch. Em was talking about finding the plants where Daniel had died and her dream. She wished she could hear how the old woman reacted to the dream talk. Most people were shocked or frightened or thought Em was making it up. Hopefully, Amelia had lived long enough to have known others in the mountains who were clairvoyant. After what Em had said this afternoon, it wouldn't do for Amelia to be a nonbeliever.

A moment later, Em came inside, looked at her mother, and announced, "I know what to do about the dreams. Amelia knows."

Carey turned around and was going to ask, but the expression on Em's face was so pleasant, she thought it was best to ask Amelia. Whatever she had said must have satisfied Em.

She said, "Good night," and disappeared into her room.

"I'm heading out to my camp. Is there anything I can help with?"

"No, I'm mostly finished. I am curious how you helped Em with the dream thing."

"Unless you have the gift of sight, what I said wouldn't make any sense to you. It's a little like knowing how a remedy works, using your faith."

Carey thought about that for a moment and then said, "Thank you."

"No worries, will my potion be ready by morning? I would like to get an early start."

"Yes, see you at breakfast?"

"That would be nice."

Amelia was not looking forward to going home. She hoped her old mule was still at the livery in the next town over the hill. He would make the long trip more bearable. He was good company; she would miss Em. She formulated a plan to write a letter to be sent to Em when she died. She wanted her to know how much she cared. Even though she would not tell her she was related to her, she could still leave all that she owned to her. After all, there was no one else to leave it to; they were are dead and buried.

CHAPTER THIRTY-NINE

Jason and Red

Jason and Red watched the slow-moving oxen pulling the freight wagons and the families of the wagon train head west away from the Pawnee Rock. They spread out across the prairie in two columns, with the livestock in between. The families walked on the insides of their wagons to shield them from possible attacks. Thanks to the presence of the sniper on the Rock, they continued safely out of sight with no incidents.

"Will they be safe all the way to the fort?" Jason asked.

Red said, "We will be following close enough that the watchers will advise against it."

"The watchers?" Jason inquired.

"The original war party has been camped along the river according to the Osage traders."

"You knew this all along. Why didn't you tell me?"

"I knew if they attacked, you would have to shoot to kill. I thought I could save you from the worry. Was it wrong of me?" Red said with genuine concern.

Jason considered this statement. Red had somehow seen into his confused soul, and it frightened him. He truly would like to avoid killing. He hoped that the Indian Wars could be avoided entirely but was beginning to doubt it.

During their encampment on Pawnee Rock, Jason had heard a driver relaying the story of the Sand Creek massacre. One hundred sixty-three women, children, and elderly Indians had been wiped out by Colonel Chivington, whom they thought was a friend to them. It had happened four years earlier but had not been forgotten by the Indians or the whites. It was one of those unforgiveable acts of war depending on your point of view. Some of the white settlers were disturbed by Chivington's actions, but just as many thought it was just what those Indians deserved. Washington was starting to encourage any actions that were good for westward expansion.

They reached Fort Larned two days after the freight wagons. Jason was astonished at how many Indians were within the fort itself. He asked Red what it meant.

"Fort Larned is a distribution site for the annuities that the treaties have provided for these tribes. So they come and go as they please. Their reservations are just south of here.

"The dangerous ones are the 'dog soldiers,' who are still roving and not under control of the Indian Agency. We have arrived in the middle of preparations to deliver annuities to the Medicine Lodge Treaty conference. We will be held up here for a few days, awaiting an armed escort to take us north to Leadville and the Rockies."

Jason was disappointed at the hold; he was uncomfortable with how crowded the fort was. All this mixed company made him quite nervous. It seemed no matter where he looked, there were groups of settlers nervously eyeing Indians. It would take one stupid move to light this powder keg, in his opinion. It didn't ease his mind at all to see the boy, John, from his luncheon on the Rock, sporting a revolver.

"Hey, John. Do you know how dangerous that can be?" Jason said, motioning to the gun.

"I couldn't believe Ma even let me carry it, but she's scared. All these Injuns."

Jason thought the safest thing to do was to give the boy a tutorial about firearm safety. So together they found a place off the fort grounds to do some target shooting. It actually relaxed Jason's nerves. John was a fairly good student and very quickly was hitting the target with some consistency. They walked back to his wagon, and Jason got another home-cooked meal and many thanks from John's concerned mother.

CHAPTER FORTY

Jason and Red

All the company at the fort, Indian and soldier alike, were preparing for the running of a horserace. Red told Jason it was a commonplace entertainment. This race was a match race between a black stallion that the Indians believed their fastest. He would race against the soldiers' pick. Everywhere Jason went, men were gathering in small groups for betting. The Indians were putting up ponies, buffalo robes, and deerskins against the silver and gold coins of the soldiers, traders, and settlers.

The atmosphere surrounding the sporting event added to the daily confusion of the fort. Even though whiskey was forbidden on a military base, Jason saw signs of drunken behavior. He suspected the suppliers must be someone within the driver's ranks. Red agreed and, on behalf of his father's company, started an investigation, and of course, he solicited Jason's assistance.

They first went to talk with some of Red's Indian friends, so Jason was able to observe them up close and personally. Only a few spoke English, so he was unable to follow much of Red's discussion. He found that he was as much a curiosity to them as they were to him. One of the Indians was gesturing to him and pointing at his rifle. Jason heard one of the others say, "Long Rifle," and all the Indians looked straight at him. It made him uncomfortable; he stood his ground but made sure Red was aware of what was happening.

Red pointed in Jason's direction and said, "This is 'Long Rifle,' he is my friend. He is also friend to all Indians who do not attack the white man." He repeated the statement in the Indian's language so all understood. Then he placed his hand on Jason's shoulder; during his speech, he had moved so he stood between Jason and the group of Indians.

Jason relaxed as the Indians lost interest in him, and the discussion turned to whiskey and who had delivered it to the fort. The Indian who was giving Red the information was a scout working for the Indian agency. He had been asked to report any drinking among the Indians to the fort commander, but the whiskey had not been made available to anyone but the soldiers, who had bribed the driver to bring it.

Jason could tell that Red was angry about what he had been told. As they walked away from the group, he was muttering under his breath. Jason thought he would let him calm down before he asked any questions. So they walked in silence.

As they walked, Jason studied on the living condition of these reservation Indians. They were dirty and looked to be destitute. These were the beggars who had been described to him when they left Independence. It was easy to understand their reluctance to live as the treaties demanded. All the promised food and supplies had not been delivered, and yet they were forced to stay near the forts to collect. They were forbidden to hunt game even to feed their families. They had become slaves to a government that didn't care if they survived and had no understanding of their culture. Between Washington and the frontier, there was more corruption than Jason had witnessed during the war. The deaths were more drawn out than an assassin's bullet, yet it still smelled like murder to Jason's mind.

Turning back to Red, he said, "Do you know who brought the whiskey?"

"Yes, but nothing can be done about it. The commanders of this fort are distributing it themselves. At least so far, none has been given to the Indians."

"What about the Indian agents, will they help?"

"No, there is only us. And anything we do could get us arrested or shot."

"So what's the plan?"

Red explained that he knew where the bulk of the whiskey had been stored. Their plan was to destroy it before it was distributed. The destruction of the stores could only appear as an accident; the army, settlers, or the Indians could not be blamed. Stampeding one of the many herds grazing around the fort and near the Indian encampment would most likely work, but directing a stampede would take skilled labor.

"Meet me where the Indian ponies graze just before dark," Red shouted over his shoulder.

"Where are you going now?"

"To find the right help, just meet me later."

Jason watched the half-breed walk away, bewildered; he thought, *How could you find help for such a job without engaging the only people in the area?* He was right that no one could be trusted. The static between all the different factions was obvious.

CHAPTER FORTY-ONE

Jason and Red

Jason arrived at the rendezvous before Red. He sat down under a small tree that persisted in growing along the edge of the grassland. There was just enough shade for one man as long as you were willing to squat low enough. If he looked in a westerly direction, he could see the outline of the Rockies. His destination, the mountains of the Colorado Territory, how would they compare to the mountains he had left behind?

Jason's mind, without his realizing it, slipped back to the last time he had sat on the trail lookout. Carey would be a mother by now and Daniel a father. He was relieved that he had not destroyed all their lives that day. How did the Rockies compare? They could never be better than the West Virginia mountains of his youth; Carey wasn't a part of them.

The rumbling of an approaching wagon interrupted his thoughts. Red had arrived accompanied by several young Indian boys and some wooden crates containing wild animals. Red explained that with the help of the boys and their pets, which ranged from jackrabbits to coyotes and, of course, there mustang ponies, he planned to stampede the herds creating mass confusion within the fort.

"What guarantees they will destroy the whiskey barrels?" Jason asked.

"None," Red replied, "that's our job."

Prior to the stampede, they would arrange the barrels so that at least a few would be trampled, but the rest they would simply break up with axes during the confusion and burn. The fort commanders would not be able to acknowledge the presence of the whiskey, so the investigation into the stampede would be limited to any other destruction.

Red explained to the boys they would need to drive the herds from the north of the fort, moving them close enough slowly that when they panicked, at least half would be forced through the open gates. Jason watched the boy's faces as Red explained the plan. They were all eager to be involved; they saw this as a brave thing. Red also explained to them the danger of the drive not just from the soldiers but also the unpredictability of the panicked herds.

The boys responded, "We are the sneakiest of all the tribe. We will be like spirits, unseen by everyone."

Red thanked them and sent them home. They would return at sunset to make their preparations and release the animals.

Jason waited until they had left and asked Red, "Who are those kids?"

"They are orphans, mostly half-breeds, like me."

"Who takes care of them?"

"They take care of each other. They are strong and brave. Their families were either killed or left the reservations, leaving them behind. Their loyalties are with each other. They are unique among the Indians."

"I hope this action doesn't get them killed," Jason said with concern.

Red snickered and said, "They are the sneakiest. They will not be seen."

They found a place near the whiskey storage area in the late afternoon. They overturned a couple of nail kegs and played a game of checkers. They positioned themselves where one of them could see the storage area and the other the open gate of the compound. As the sun was setting, three of the company drivers rounded the corner with tin cups in their hands. When they saw Red and Jason, they stopped short. Red and Jason watched as they had a discussion among themselves, then one of the men approached.

"Good evening, gents," he started. "Would you be interested in a drink?"

To Jason's great surprise, Red looked up at the man and said, "Yeah, Jack, sounds good."

Jack waved his buddies over; they produced extra cups, which they handed to Jason and Red. Jack filled all their cups and proposed a toast. Jason was astonished as these men raised their glasses to toast the half-breed, who was their known enemy. Jason almost laughed; it seemed so ludicrous, but he followed Red's lead and actually enjoyed his first sip of whiskey since he was in St. Louis.

Over the shoulders of these men, Jason saw the herd slowly moving in the direction of the fort. He gestured to Red, who started walking away with the group of men in the opposite direction, laughing and saying good night until they turned the corner.

When Red returned, they finished off the drinks, sat the cups on the barrels they had been sitting on, and backed up against the wall. The herd was gaining momentum; they could see the heads bouncing, and the noise of hundreds of hooves had reached the fort. They waited for the first shout within the fort and began smashing whiskey barrels. They overturned several kegs just before the animals started down the alley where they were stored. Jason and Red plastered themselves against the wall of the building and watched as the stampeding herd destroyed everything in its path.

Jason watched closely at the gate for any sign of the "sneakiest" Indians and was not disappointed that he saw no one. He did see some coyotes loping away as if someone was calling them. Jason and Red joined the soldiers and other occupants of the fort and helped gather the cattle and horses. Except for the narrow alleyway that was in a direct line from the front gate, the destruction was minimal.

Red and Jason had to walk away quickly when a group of men gathered at the whiskey storage; they didn't want their laughter to give up their secret. The entertainment of the day's race would not be spoiled by drunken rivalries sparking a war at Fort Larned. The gents would have to be satisfied with a lesser evil; homemade cider would be available to all in small quantities.

CHAPTER FORTY-TWO

The Race

The morning of the race, Jason heard several drivers discussing the destruction of the whiskey. Some of them complained while others thought the absence of whiskey would make the day more sporting. Many of them talked about an incident that had occurred at a race day in New Mexico that had sparked a full-out war with the normally peaceful Navajo. Apparently, someone had tampered with the bridle of the Navajo's pony, which resulted in the loss of the race. When the Navajo called for a rerun, the all-soldier panel of judges refused. Many of the bets went unpaid, and the shooting of an intoxicated Indian resulted in an attack upon the Indian encampments, killing women and children.

At least this race had a representative for the Indians on the judge's panel. The fort's Indian agency had asked Red to serve, and he had agreed. The fact that he was a half-breed seemed to have been ignored. Red told Jason, because he was neither white nor Indian, everyone expected him to be fair to both sides, but he just followed his own beliefs no matter whom it affected. The race would be won by the fastest horse, and he hoped it would be the Indians' horse, because they were more likely to wage a complaint than the soldiers. He didn't want to be the middleman, but he accepted the position to keep the peace.

All of Jason's worries were banished as the big black stallion belonging to Lone Eagle galloped easily across the finish line at least three lengths in front of Major Johnson's chestnut.

There was some banter about a rematch, but sportsmanship prevailed, and all bets were covered.

Major Johnson had lost his chestnut horse to Lone Eagle, but he had no complaints as, technically, it wasn't his horse; it belonged to the army—a fact that would go undetected for months after Major Johnson had gone east and the chestnut and Lone Eagle had gone west.

The morning following the race the freight wagons along with the assigned military escort left Fort Larned headed west to the town of Pueblo. Red and Jason rode on top of a load of machinery. It was covered with a tarp and mostly flat, so for the first couple of miles, they stretched out on their bedrolls and caught up on their sleep. They had been unable to get much real rest since before the stampede.

The presence of the mounted and armed soldiers allowed Jason to relax. The wagons were now on a well-traveled road, and a bit of rain had dampened everything, so the dust wasn't bad either. They forded the Arkansas River near La Junta and continued along the valley road to Pueblo. Jason awoke when the wagon he was sleeping on began to climb an incline. He sat up to see mountains unlike anything he had ever experienced. The highest peaks were some distance away, but they were indeed massive as they rose to meet the blue sky.

"So there they are," Red said. "I see by your gaping mouth they are more than you expected."

Jason stopped himself from answering. What he was feeling was much too personal. Seeing these mountains had brought a million thoughts of home erupting into his brain so quickly and overwhelmingly that he was on the verge of screaming. No one who did not know the Jason of his youth would understand. Carey would understand.

Red laughed and added, "This is just the beginning!"

Jason stared at the mountains and thought of home.

CHAPTER FORTY-THREE

Em

In the weeks following Amelia's departure, Carey saw a change in Em. She seemed to be a little less serious about everyday things. She sought out all the children visiting with their mothers who came to see Carey for remedies or just to visit. They played silly, childish games, something that had never interested her before Amelia's talk. Carey was relieved and happy to see her be a child. When she asked Em about the change in her behavior, Em said, "Amelia said most things that happen to people around you are going to happen whether you foresee it or not. Stop anticipating and just let it unfold."

Carey wasn't sure she understood, but if it was helping Em feel more normal, then who was she to worry? Her own dreams were not prophetic, so she was never waiting to see them happen for real. She felt a little guilty that her dreams were more about Jason than Daniel. Since Daniel's death, they had sometimes appeared together. Even in those dreams, Jason was a clearer image than Daniel. Carey hated to admit that it was most likely because she still didn't think Jason was dead. No returning soldiers had ever reported knowing what happened to him. In the last letters she received, he had talked about going north for training. She had heard rumors that he was used as a sharpshooter, which was feasible because he was a good shot. It sounded like a safer job than infantry or cavalry, but then she really didn't know much about fighting. If it had been safer then he would have returned, if he was alive.

On Sunday mornings, Carey and Em would walk hand in hand around the farm, inspecting the sheep herds and gathering herbs. They would pass the spot on the creek where Jason had first promised his love to Carey. Em always wondered why they would hesitate at this spot, but she never asked. She did notice the quiet mood that fell over her mother when they passed.

Some days, when her mother allowed, she would wander along the creek alone. When Em found the tree with her mother's initials carved alongside another's, she did ask. Her mother told her when she was a young girl, she had fallen in love with a boy; his name was Jason.

When Em asked for more information about the boy, her mother had said it was all in the past and best forgotten. Em didn't press her for more that day. She did know that her mother was being secretive, and that was unusual.

A few days later, Carey sent Em to the Baxters to deliver some sheepskins. She packed the skins on Aslan's back since they were too bulky and heavy for Em to carry without help. Em led the horse merrily along, whistling at the beautiful day. She was excited about seeing the Baxters; they had been like grandparents to her. Em had decided to ask Mary Baxter about the boy Jason. She had lived in these parts long enough to have known him.

"Good morning, Mrs. Baxter, I have brought the skins for you."

"Well, good day to you, little one," Mrs. Baxter answered sweetly. "I'm surprised you were allowed to come on your own."

"I talked Mom into it," Em said with enthusiasm.

"Tie Aslan there and come on in. I can get Jeb to unload him while we talk."

"Good, 'cause that's what I came to do."

"All right then, what shall we talk about?" Mary Baxter said, thinking what a precocious child Em can be.

Em looked directly at Mrs. Baxter and fairly demanded, "Tell me about Jason."

Mary Baxter looked at her with an astonished look. She was quite surprised that Em hadn't heard the story of Jason Emerson.

She thought for a long minute before speaking then said, "Have you asked your mother about Jason?"

"She would only tell me she had loved him as a young girl. It's not enough. I need to know more."

"If she didn't tell you more, I'm thinking you should ask her, not me."

"I think it makes her sad to talk about him, so please tell me," Em pleaded.

Mrs. Baxter was touched by the child's concern and thought there would be no harm in telling her at least part of the story.

"Jason Emerson and your mother grew up in these mountains. They were inseparable. Your great-grandmother said they were destined to be together. The war took that from them. He left and never returned. Your mother married Daniel and that was that. If you need to know more, you will have to ask your mother."

Em thanked Mary, jumped off the porch onto, Aslan's back and waved over her shoulder as she trotted up the trail toward home. She rode until she was out of sight of the Baxter cabin and then turned into the woods, making her own trail in the direction of the tree with the initials. She now knew she was named for her mother's childhood lover, but she believed Daniel was her father.

The short ride to the tree gave her little time to decide what her next move should be; she allowed Aslan to graze nearby and sat down by the tree. Em had gone through the box of tin types and keepsakes that her mother kept under her bed. There were only three pictures. One was of her great-grandmother, who had passed shortly after her birth. One was Daniel all decked out in his soldiering clothes before he had lost his arm. The third picture was a man she had never seen. He was also in a uniform, but it was different from Daniel's. This man had fought for the Union. Now she knew that this man was Jason Emerson, whose name she had been given. In the bottom of the trunk was Carey's wedding dress, neatly folded. Em had left it undisturbed; she knew she could not put it back without her mother knowing.

Em had only heard her mother speak his name one time; Carey and Daniel were arguing. They only argued when Daniel had been to town to meet with the other amputees. Em was young, and most of the conversation wasn't loud enough to come through the wall into her room, but she definitely heard the name Jason. Afterward Daniel had left the house, and in the morning, he came in from the direction of the barn. Em had watched while he asked Carey's forgiveness, and then they hugged and Em never heard them argue again, at least not that involved the name Jason.

Carey's explanation of him as someone she loved as a young girl didn't quite fit with Mrs. Baxter's story. She may have loved him as a young girl, but obviously, she must have loved him when he went off to war. Em did not want to cause her mother any pain, but she needed to know more; she would keep investigating.

Over the next few weeks, Em inquired of everyone she met over a certain age about Jason Emerson. Of course, some people remembered him, but no one she talked to knew him. She had just about given up hope when an old man from near Romney came to visit the Baxters. Just by chance, Em was having lunch with Mary when he arrived. Em noticed he wore an old tattered soldier's cap. It was so worn, she couldn't tell if it was blue or gray.

"Which side did you fight on?" she inquired.

The man looked down at little Em and, with a little hesitation, said, "Why?"

"I'm trying to find out what happened to a man from around these parts who never came back. He was a Yankee."

"War's over. Why do you need to know? It's best forgotten."

"Em, did you talk to your mother about all this?" Mary Baxter interrupted with concern.

"She won't talk about him except to say she loved him as a boy. You know that's not the whole truth."

The old man looked at his friend Mary and whispered, "This man's name Jason?"

Em said, "Yes, that is his name. Did you know him?"

The old man was amazed that she had heard him, but he knew now he had said too much. He would have no choice but to tell his story. He had come to this area to tell his story, but not to a little child. He had come in search of the Carey that Jason had told him about in the woods on the mountain.

"Are you Carey's child?" he inquired. He knew the answer; the age was right, and she fit the description of her mother that Jason had told him. "After lunch you will take me to your mother."

"I think she will be angry about this," Em said with hesitation.

"We'll just tell her I came inquiring about Jason. Will that help?" and he smiled.

Em smiled from ear to ear and said, "Yes!"

When they had finished lunch, Em took Mr. Thompson by the hand; he told her to call him Jonathan, and they headed up the road to the cove. She was still concerned about how all of this would affect her mother, but now she would hear the whole story. She had been seeing the arrival of a man in her dreams; maybe Jonathan was that man, but he seemed too old. Her dreams were always unclear. Amelia said the fuzzy ones were more likely to be prophetic, whatever that meant, Em remembered.

When they reached the bottom pasture, Em cut across the fields so she could be at the cabin before Mr. Thompson. Carey had seen someone approaching and was standing on the porch, drying her hands on a towel. She could tell by his gait he was elderly. Carey assumed it was someone coming for a remedy and went back in the cabin.

Em burst into the cabin, banging the door against the wall, which always irritated Carey. She spun around to reprimand her, but the expression of joy on her face made the angry words stop at her lips.

Instead she said, "My goodness, what has you all lit up?"

Em grabbed her by the hand and, dragging her back onto the porch, said, "That man Jonathan knows where Jason is!"

The man was making his way slowly up the hill to the cabin when, Carey grasping the words that Em had spoken, collapsed into the closest chair. Em was frightened by the reaction and wasn't sure what she should say or do. Several minutes passed, and Carey sat in stunned silence.

"Em, go to your room. Go to your room, now!"

Em wanted to refuse but the look on her mother's face sent her scurrying for the safety of her room. She lay back on the bed and tried to remain very still. Hopefully, the words from the porch would creep into her room through the open window. Surely, after Jonathan left, she would hear the story from her mother.

Jonathan was out of breath when he reached the porch. He sat down on the first step and waited a few minutes before speaking. As he looked out over the farm and the grazing sheep, he thought of his lost family. Carey moved in the chair behind him but didn't speak.

He turned and said, "I seemed to have stirred up a mess. I should not have inquired about Jason in front of the child."

"The mention of his name was certainly enough to get her started."

"I'm sorry. My intention was only to inquire about him and find out if he had been in touch with you."

"No, he never returned after the war," Carey said with a deep remorse.

"He told me he came here, but you were living with another man and you were pregnant."

Carey looked at Jonathan with distress. He realized his coming was a very big mistake. He had opened a very deep wound that had had time to heal. He had just wanted to meet Jason's Carey. He had told Jason to come and hear the story from Carey's side, but he had never returned. He must have continued to fight and kill until coming home was impossible.

"How, how did you know him?" Carey asked hesitantly.

Jonathan told her the entire story from the shooting at the ferry to their meeting in the mountains. Carey was torn apart by the tragedy of it all. If only he had come down and learned the truth about her pregnancy and Daniel's sacrifice to help her. She thought how horrible for him to go to his death, not knowing the truth. She asked Jonathan if he thought Jason could be alive.

"There is a possibility. The job he was doing is less dangerous than being in the fray, and when I saw him, he had decided coming home would be worse for all of you. Carey, he was very off-center about all the killings he had been asked to do."

"I could have forgiven anything, but not coming home. He promised."

Jonathan could see her pain and didn't want to add to it, but he said, "He did come home!"

"There was an explanation. Daniel and my grandmother went to their graves protecting it. Em cannot know that Daniel was not her father."

Jonathan then listened while Carey told him her side of the story. She explained that she had only relayed this story to Daniel and her grandmother. She said the only reason to tell him was, if by chance he ever saw Jason again, then he could send him home. She would be waiting for him to fulfill his promise. Any darkness that he held in his soul she could release with all the love she had carried with her for the duration of the war. She had married Daniel to give Em a family and loved him until he was lost, but Jason had always been foremost in her heart.

CHAPTER FORTY-FOUR

Alice

Alice had been best friends with Jim and John growing up around St. Louis. She had always seen herself married to one or the other, but the war had made that decision for her. They had been married several months when Jim told her the circumstances of John's death. As he relayed the story, she tried not to show how horrific it was; she was unable to understand how it could have happened. There had been so little fighting in and around St. Louis; the mail service wasn't good, so news of the front had been vague and seldom unbiased. She knew Jim was telling the truth, but it was very hard to imagine what he and John had gone through.

Since Jim's return, he had gone through several weeks of depressive behavior. At first Alice had thought it had something to do with his job or his dad, but now she knew it was the war and John's death. She was so glad that she had suggested they get married and put all of it behind them. Jim finally opening up to her about John had provided perfect timing for telling him about the baby. He had also explained how he and Jason had become to be such good friends.

The following morning, she walked down to the Lindell Hotel and invited Jim's father to dinner.

"I have a dinner meeting with a stage agent," James McCrea said

"Bring him along," Alice said without hesitation. She didn't want to put the announcement off for another day; besides, Jim's father was always entertaining someone for dinner. "Cooking for four is just as easy as three," she added.

"Well, if you insist," James said. Alice noticed the twinkle in his eye but couldn't detect the meaning.

"Dinner will be served at seven thirty, and I expect you to be prompt."

"Yes, ma'am," James said with mock sarcasm and watched Alice go with a smile. He had suspected, but he knew the look of a pregnant woman; after all, he had raised a big family. The grandbabies would help fill the void of losing his sons and his wife. James was thrilled that Jim had made it home and had stayed, especially since his dream had always been to go west and farm. Alice had changed all that; he did feel a little guilty in that he suspected if John had lived, Jim would have left. The war had caused so many bad things; he was thankful for the way this had turned out. Alice was a good woman and would be a great mother.

Alice stopped by the market and the vegetable stand on the way back to the house. This dinner needed to be special, so she was going to prepare all of Jim's favorites, finishing with a rhubarb pie. She was using an old recipe that she had found folded in between the pages of Jim's mother's cookbook; along the bottom, someone had written "Jim's favorite." Alice hoped she could do it right; she had never baked a rhubarb pie, but she figured it couldn't be too different from an apple pie.

Alice spent the afternoon preparing. She set the table for four. She baked the pie and sat it on the windowsill to cool. Throughout the day, everything had gone according to her plan, and dinner was coming along nicely. She would have time to dress leisurely before Jim would arrive.

Jim came home from the dispatch office every day around 6:00 p.m., and today was no different.

"Alice, I'm home," he shouted from the front door as usual.

That was her cue; she left their room and stopped at the head of the stairs. When Jim looked up and saw her, the expression on his face made her fully aware of how much he loved her. She was bursting to tell him her news, but her plan was a grand announcement over a lovely dinner. Jim didn't wait for her to descend the stairs; he met her halfway, giving her a big McCrea hug.

"It looks like I had better clean up for dinner. What's the occasion? I ran into Da' at the hotel. He was ordering a bottle of champagne."

"Can't say why he bought champagne. He's bringing some stage agent with him for dinner. Maybe it has something to do with that," Alice answered. She had no clue what it could mean, but champagne would top off her dinner nicely. Her special occasion had just gotten more special.

Da' and his business associate arrived right on time, and Jim joined them for a before-dinner drink while Alice and Maltilda were finishing in the kitchen. Alice invited the men into the dining room. Maltilda served at seven thirty sharp. Randall, the stage agent, was thrilled to have a home-cooked meal. Apparently, his trip out from New York had been quite an adventure, one of the last mail runs on his stage line. He explained how the completion of the Transcontinental Railroad would be the end of the long stage lines. He had been sent west to decide which short-distance routes could be kept open.

"What will be the criteria for keeping them open?" asked James.

"Profit," Randall quickly replied. "Some of the shorter lines don't need mail contracts to make money. They carry passengers regularly enough."

Jim asked, "So the lines that don't make money will just be closed?"

"No, they will be sold."

"Who will buy?" Jim inquired.

"Anyone who sees a way to make them profitable. With the equipment, you could do a good local freight service. An investor just has to make sure the business is there."

James said, "Sounds risky."

"There are certain lines that are sure things. I'll know more after I've been to California and back," Randall announced. "I've been instructed to travel all the lines that have been showing a profit so I can estimate their worth. The others will just stop running, and the equipment will be sold off or repurposed."

"Well, sounds like an ambitious task and a lot of bouncing around from here to California. I'm glad to be home in St. Louis," Jim said, smiling at Alice.

Alice smiled back and rang for the main course. Matilda appeared at the door with the beautiful roast surrounded by steaming vegetables. She placed it in front of Jim, who sat at the end of the table opposite his wife. Alice was so pleased at the expressions of her guests and thankful that her evening was going as smoothly as planned.

When the dishes were cleared and before the dessert was served, Alice stood and cleared her throat. She had instructed Matilda to hold the dessert until after her announcement, which she had shared with her while they prepared dinner. The men stopped their casual conversation and looked at her. Jim looked afraid for a moment and started to ask what was happening.

"Jim, I prepared this lovely dinner for us to announce our first child."

Jim stared at Alice in complete silence. James smiled from ear to ear and produced the bottle of champagne from under the table. Randall smiled in amusement at Jim. He sat dumbfounded in his chair with a blank expression. Alice started to panic.

Why doesn't he say something? How can he be so shocked? After all, we had talked about a family.

Jim jumped out of his seat just as his father popped the champagne; he was at Alice's side in less than the time it took for the bubbling liquid to pour onto the table cloth. Alice was wrapped in the best McCrea hug ever as Jim's father looked on with pride. Randall took over the pouring of the champagne. Matilda served the rhubarb pie.

When they had settled back in their seats, Alice took a taste of the rhubarb pie. It was so sour, she thought she had done something wrong. Jim and his Da' were both talking about how great it tasted. Alice thought they were just being nice to the pregnant woman.

"The thing that makes rhubarb great with champagne is that great sourness."

Alice laughed and said, "You mean it's supposed to taste like this? I had never baked a rhubarb pie before."

"Alice, once again you have amazed me," Da' said. "This taste just like my grandmother's recipe."

"I found it in the old cookbook. It said 'Jim's favorite.'"

James cocked his head sideways and said, "Yep, that would be me!"

Alice laughed again.

"I'm just glad it goes with champagne and baby announcements."

Jim smiled at his lovely wife and began to look forward to being a father.

CHAPTER FORTY-FIVE

Jason

Jason knew he could not leave immediately he would need to fulfill his obligations to the freight company and to Red. To complete his two-year contract, he would make a few more crossings from St. Louis to Colorado Springs and back again. The final stages of these crossings involved traveling along the foothills, making deliveries to the mining towns whose machinery was lashed to the wagons. It would be a tedious task for him and slow going, but the closer they got to Colorado Springs, the less freight they would be carrying. Guarding the wagons against attack also became more challenging. There were a lot of ambush spots on the mountain trails. The Indians were less of a threat, but the gangs of outlaws who hid out in these mountains were ruthless.

Red and Jason rode horseback from early morning until noon, scouting the trail ahead. At noon they would ride back to the wagons and have lunch, sitting on top of some flat place on the freight. Occasionally a driver would pull his wagon off the road and wait while he was unloaded before resuming. The material from these wagons would be carried off on smaller wagons and taken directly to an individual mine site. As the wagons got lighter, the pace of the convoy would quicken, but oxen only moved so fast.

Red and Jason had their lunch on a stopped wagon and conversed with the miners who were unloading. Some of these men had been in these mountains alone for so long that they weren't very talkative. They were eager to get back to their claims. Jason read that part of their silence was worry that while they were picking up equipment, someone would steal from them.

Some were veterans who had come in search of gold. None of them had brought family, so with all the distrust among them, Jason could feel the loneliness.

They were different from the settlers Jason had met; they came for the gold and silver, and once they had it, they would go back where they came from originally. If they spoke at all, it was to ask about news from home. Most had come from west of the Mississippi River, but occasionally Jason would catch the familiar accent of the Commonwealth of Virginia.

"Hey, where y'all coming from?" one of the younger men asked.

Jason answered, "Near Romney, West Virginia originally."

"Don't you know there is only West Virginia now? You all seceded from Virginia at the beginning of the War Between the States."

"Don't you know that war is over and better forgot?" Jason retorted.

"Well, that's a fact, and that's easy to do way out here in the Rockies. But I'll be heading home soon. I have more than enough to call it quits. I'm going to take the train!"

"How long you been gone?"

"I left before the fighting started. My daddy thought I should fight for the Rebs. It was easier to come out here than disappoint that man. I had five brothers. They're all dead fightin' for the South. My father is less disappointed in me than when I left. Hopefully, a successful mine will make him forgive me."

The young man started up the trace to his mine and shouted over his shoulder, "From what I've seen, you are one of the lucky ones!"

Jason had never thought he was lucky to have survived the war. It had always been unlucky that he had to fight at all. This exchange made him think about all the men he had passed on the streets of Washington the weeks following the signing of the treaty. He wondered how many were still lost and realized he was lucky indeed.

HOME

The return trip to St. Louis was less eventful, possibly because the freight traveling east was not worth the risk of stealing unless you were building a house. The lumber loads were lighter and less bulky than the machinery, easier to balance on the flatbeds. Some of the older drivers told stories of shipping massive logs before the lumber mills were opened near the springs.

Jason had received a letter from Jim. His excitement came through in his writing. Jim and his young wife, Alice, had conceived a child. He or she would be born very close to the time Jason would be back in St. Louis. Jason was surprised at how quickly they had started a family. He remembered how he and Carey had planned when they would start a family. They had talked about how "someday" they would have a big family. The thought depressed him. "Someday" was almost inconceivable after what had happened to them, but if Carey would forgive him and since he had forgiven her, at least he could go back to his mountains. Jason shook his head and thought, *What makes you think Daniel will give her up?*

This thought made him waver from his decision; perhaps going home even after all this time could not be worth the pain. Until now Jason hadn't considered Daniel in his return. When he got back to St. Louis, he would write to Daniel. He would need his side of the story as well. He knew the loss of his arm was what had brought him home from the war early, but how did he end up with Carey?

The freight train had reached Pawnee Rock and camped along the river for some repairs. Jason had taken up his lookout position on the rock, not because of any real threat but to find a quieter place to think. There was still a steady stream of settlers trudging along the trail below. He counted six hundred wagons over the course of the two days he camped on the rock. Most of the hostiles were being driven away by troopers or rounded up and taken to reservations. Red said the old way of life was being systematically destroyed, and for the first time in his life, he was ashamed of his heritage, both Indian and white.

Jason spent the next few days catching his journal up, rereading what he had written and discarding some of the blacker entries. He was glad to see that the farther he had gotten from Washington, the less often he had written from depression or loneliness. He realized that he had finally accepted what Captain Humphrey's had explained about war and being a soldier. He had, in fact, let the flow take him away from the past. Now he could see a future; now he needed to figure a way to finance that future.

CHAPTER FORTY-SIX

Jason

By the time the wagon train moved on, Jason had an investment plan. He had heard that with the completion of the railroad, the long-distance stage lines and the pony express would be selling out. What if he could invest his earnings in a shorter-distance stage line that would and could continue to operate at a profit? When he arrived in St. Louis, Jim's dad might be able to introduce him to the right people; he met people from the east every day at his hotel.

With a plan formulated, he mailed a return letter to Jim; the pony express would have it there several weeks before the freight wagons would pull into St. Louis. Jason was surprised at how comforting it was to know Jim and Alice would be waiting for him when he arrived. He had begun to think of them as family, and he was excited about being Uncle Jason.

Traveling east from Pawnee Rock to Westport, Jason realized that during his trip west, he had been so consumed with his protection detail that he had witnessed very little of the beauty of the land. He had seen the vastness of the prairie but none of the beautiful detail of it. Now that he understood the nature of the dangers from Indians or outlaws, he could quickly analyze the possibility of attack, then he could use all his keen observation skills to see his immediate surroundings. It had a calming effect; he knew he still preferred the mountain forests of his youth, but the land west of the Mississippi had its appeal.

His idea that being on the plains was comparable to being on the ocean did apply to its flatness and the distance to the horizon. The color was not blue but golden; the tall grass undulated with the wind. The wind changed direction, often creating ripples and contrast in the grasses. Using his gun scope, Jason was able to pick out birds balancing on the small scrub bushes interspersed in the grass. They bobbed back and forth, trying to maintain their perch despite the wind. If Jason watched closely, the line of the grass was occasionally broken up by a bounding coyote in pursuit of small prey or small herds of deer and antelope grazing.

On the way west, his gaze was always out and away from the track. He had only acknowledged the terrain when it got rough enough to feel in his seat bones. He had never seen any of the roadside debris. The piles of bleached bones scattered along the road were disturbing. They were mostly oxen and other livestock, but occasionally, with his trained eye, Jason recognized the remains of a human; unburied human most likely indicated an Indian rather than a settler. Certain more difficult sections of the trail revealed numerous graves.

When Jason inquired concerning the graves, the drivers said, "Most of those graves are from the early crossings. You know, before the watering holes were well marked and, for that matter, the trails."

A second driver added, "The bones became trail markers along with the discarded belongings of the westward-bound families."

The graves reminded Jason of his walk back to Romney during the war. In the east, there were rows of graves near all the major battles. He had read recently where some folks had been able to retrieve the bodies of their relatives and return them to their homes. He wondered if settlers would return to these sites, but without gravestones, how would they know if the body was the right one?

Would they take them home to the east or home to the west?

Jason watched the backs of the plodding oxen from his perch on a pile of lumber atop one of the bigger cargo wagons. He could see the first wagon in the train ten wagons ahead and then look over his shoulder and see all the way to the last of the wagons ten wagons behind. Twenty wagons stretched out over about two miles. He raised his gaze and did his hourly sweep of the surroundings to reassure himself there was no threat at this juncture. Red was riding back along the line of wagons. He stopped when he came alongside Jason's location.

Raising his hand, he shouted, "Come down and join me. I want to show you something."

Jason climbed down, untied and mounted his horse from the back of the wagon, and joined Red as he rode off toward a nearby rise.

"Where we headed?" Jason called when he caught up to Red.

"Patience" was Red's only reply.

They cantered along side by side when they crested the rise; spread out in front of them was one of the most inviting scenes Jason had witnessed since leaving Denver—a ribbon of greenery following the line of Big John Creek as it meandered its way down to a larger stand of trees. Jason was impressed with the beauty of this place.

"This is the place I consider home," Red said. "Except for its place in Indian history, it would be perfect."

"What is this place called?"

"Council Grove, it is where the first treaty was signed. It allowed for the unmolested passage of the whites through Osage land, my mother's people."

Jason wasn't sure what his response should be, so he remained silent and took in the beauty of the place. Red seemed to be doing the same. Jason knew he could never understand Red's emotions when it came to Indian affairs. All of what he had seen and heard on this trip went directly back to the politics. The young United States government was greedy and corrupt. Indians were not considered worthy of humanitarian treatment; they got in the way of economic development. Western expansion had trampled the rights of the Native Americans and changed the course of their lives, and it had all started at Council Grove in the Kansas Territories.

"Sorry," Red said, "I didn't mean to put a cloud over this place. It's still my favorite eastward view."

"I can certainly see why," Jason responded.

The wagons had caught up to their position and were slowly descending toward the creek crossing. This crossing put them 110 miles from Westport. The pony express riders had reported a great many improvements to the road from Westport to St. Louis. Once the wagons reached Westport, Jason and Red would ride ahead on horseback. They would reach St. Louis ahead of them to start preparations at the supply depot.

CHAPTER FORTY-SEVEN

Jason

When the wagons were two days' ride from St. Louis, Red and Jason rode ahead to prepare the shipping yards for the arrival of the lumber and other freight coming in from Denver. The drivers would help with the unloading, but Red's father and the staff at the depot would be on hand to assist. Then, the drivers who had been gone for months could get home to their families that much quicker. Jason was anticipating his reunion with Jim, whom he knew would be full of questions about the west.

Red said, "You should take the train."

"What?" Jason asked, lost in his thoughts.

"You should take the train. It leaves from Denver regularly. When you finish your third trip to Denver, your contract will be filled."

"What a good idea. Can I afford it?"

"I can hook you up with the Pinkerton Agency. They hire guards for the trains."

"The Pinkerton Agency operates out here?"

"Since the completion of the intercontinental railroad, yes."

"Why do they need guards?"

"Train robbers."

Jason liked the idea of getting home quickly but wasn't sure working for the Pinkerton Agency would make the trip enjoyable. However, if he could arrive in St. Louis with all his earnings from the freight trips plus some from the train ride, he could go home to West Virginia in style. If the investment plan worked, he could be quite well-to-do. It might not impress Carey, but it couldn't hurt.

Jason had begun to think about how to go home. It wasn't like he could just walk up to their cabin and say hello. After all, he had been gone for more than six years. He had written a letter to Daniel in his head but had yet to put pen to paper. He couldn't find a way to ask Daniel the circumstances without sounding accusatory and angry. He knew his love for Carey was just as strong as before. She must have believed him dead to have succumbed to Daniel's advances.

Can I forgive her? Should I forgive her?

"If we keep the pace up, we can have dinner at the Lindell Hotel tonight. I think we've earned a drink, a hot bath, and a feather bed on the company," said Red.

"Sounds great," Jason responded.

"You deserve a bonus. No losses from Indian attacks, thanks to Long Rifle."

"You believe it made a difference, having me along?" Jason asked.

"It's the first run in four years without the loss of any lives!"

Jason felt a wave of pride. He hadn't realized the effect his skills had on the trip. It made him think of Captain Humphrey again, and it put a positive slant on his soldier training. The killing of the deer had led to the saving of lives. He had found a way to keep the assassinations from taking over his soul and using his sharpshooter expertise in a positive way.

Jim was standing on the loading docks when Jason and Red rode into the yard. Red and Jim exchanged greetings, and Red entered the office to speak to his father and boss. Jason stuck his hand out awkwardly, and young Jim grabbed him and gave him his own version of the McCrea bear hug. Jason relaxed, laughed, and returned his hug. Within minutes, the year's separation was completely behind them, and just as Jason suspected, he was bombarded with questions.

Jason and Red headed to the Lindell. Jim would meet them later for a drink before heading home to Alice. Jason had to promise to have dinner with them the next evening and stay with them while he was in town no matter how long. Jason didn't know how long the freighters would be in St. Louis, but Jim assured him it didn't matter. Alice would not allow him to stay at the hotel.

CHAPTER FORTY-EIGHT

Carey and Em

After Jonathan's visit, Carey was hopeful that Jason had survived the war, but she wasn't sure if it would be good for her to believe he would ever come home. She had eliminated that possibility from her future when she had accepted Daniel as a father for Em. She wasn't sure that even as resilient as Em was, she could accept another man into their home. Carey decided that if Em continued to investigate Jason, she needed to get her facts straight. She also knew she would have to recount her story to Jason in its entirety. He would have to agree to keep her secret just as Daniel, Grandmother, and now Johnathan had agreed. She also knew that the more people she told, the possibility of Em learning the truth about her conception became probable.

After talking with Carey, Jonathan had promised to keep the entire story to himself, with the exception of Jason. Jonathan had admitted to Carey that the possibility of him running in to Jason again was very slim. Their first meeting had been totally by accident. As he headed back to his mountain farm near Romney, the thought did occur to him that he could go in search of Jason. He knew that he had been in Washington at the end of the war. Some of his war connections had known the sharpshooter while he worked on the security details.

Em had expected her mother to tell her the rest of the Jason Emerson saga, but she was even more secretive or at least evasive after Jonathan had left. She couldn't understand. During her inquiries around the mountains, she had found out that Daniel and Jason were also childhood friends. In fact, she knew that they and her mom had played together along their creek. Why was she excluding her?

Carey did not realize how much her efforts to protect Em from the truth of things was affecting the child until several days later. She had been working in the office since lunchtime and lost track of time. She had left Em playing on the porch of the house, but she was nowhere to be seen. In the house, she found a note on the counter; it said, "Gone to Daddy." Carey walked down to his gravesite. She could hear Em's crying as she approached.

In between sobs, she heard Em, "Daddy, please help me. I want to know about Mommy's first love. I think he's coming, and I want him to love me too."

Carey stopped in her tracks.

"I think he's coming." What a strange thing for her to say. "I want him to love me too." Carey realized, from Em's point of view, all of this was nothing like what she felt. She also realized that all the deception was about her shame; except for Em learning that Daniel wasn't her real father, none of it mattered.

Carey knelt down next to Em and gave her a hug.

"Em, I am so sorry. I didn't realize how upsetting this has been for you. Can you forgive me?"

"Mom, please tell me how this is all connected to me."

"I think you already know most of the story, but I will fill in the gaps," Carey said quietly.

Other than the actual rape itself, Carey relayed the entire story to Em. Carey would let her believe that Daniel was her real father, like all the townspeople did. She did tell her that her great-grandmother had predicted that she and Jason were destined to be together forever. Carey looked at Em and waited for her response.

"Do you think he still loves you?" Em asked.

"We won't know until he gets here, "Carey answered.

"Well, he is coming!" said Em. "That's my prediction."

"If you say so, but let's not let it be between us anymore."

"Will he love me too?" Em said.

"Of course, he will. He fell in love with me when I wasn't much older than you."

They walked hand in hand back toward the cabin in silence. They were both lost in their thoughts. Carey imagined how it would feel to have Jason back in her life. And then, she thought how absurd it was to even consider his return. Where could he have been all these years?

Em thought of Amelia and her explanation about prophetic dreams. Sometimes it was up to the dreamer to get a thing to happen. She believed Jason was coming home so she could have a whole family again. All she had to do now was wait.

CHAPTER FORTY-NINE

Alice, Jim, and Jay

The baby arrived in March. The timing couldn't have been more perfect for Jason. The freight wagons had finally been loaded that very afternoon. He had been living in Jim and Alice's home in the spare bedroom, which had been transformed into the nursery daily over the last few weeks. Jason didn't mind a bit, but he was ready to move into the Lindell Hotel for his last few days in town. Jim was at the depot when Alice went into labor. Maltilda had interrupted his packing to send Jason to collect him.

"You go collect Mr. Jim, but don't you hurry. This usually takes awhile," she said.

"I'll gather up my things and take the buggy. Will I have time to drop things off at the Lindell?"

"Oh sure, like I said, these things take time."

Jim loaded the buggy and drove with a little haste to the hotel. When he arrived, James was in the lobby. He watched Jason cross to the desk, give instruction to the desk clerk, and head for the door.

"Hey, Jason, where're you going in such a hurry?"

"It's Alice. The baby's comin'! I've been sent for Jim."

"Well, stop by on your way back and pick up Grandpa," James said with a smile.

Jason waved and drove off. Jim was standing with several drivers, including Red, outside the office door. They were in a heated discussion about something, but when Jim saw Jason's face, he knew.

He left the other men standing there, staring at his back, and ran toward the buggy.

Jason got them turned around and headed back to the Lindell. Jim started firing questions at Jason faster than he could answer them. Mainly because he didn't have any answers. When he stopped at the Lindell, Jim hollered, "Why are we stopping?"

Before Jason could answer, James bounded into the buggy, and they were off again. Even though Matilda had indicated no hurry, Jason felt compelled to drive recklessly fast. When they arrived at the house, Jim sprinted to the front door. James laughed and walked with Jason. He talked about the day his first child had arrived. Jason was excited for Jim and Alice but a little saddened by the fact that this was an experience he had only considered with Carey.

When they entered the house, Jim was sitting alone in the front room with a cup of tea. Matilda left the room, shaking her head and chuckling.

"I told you not to hurry."

James sat down next to Jim and said, "Now we wait. They never come until they come."

Jason refused the tea and asked Jim what the discussion at the depot was all about.

Jim looked at him with a confused expression and then explained that the drivers were concerned about the crossing; the Indians were rebelling again.

"It can't be any different than it has been, can it?"

"I wasn't aware that it had ever changed," Jim said blandly.

Jason left the house with the intention of going to the freight office to talk with Red. James caught him at the door and said, "Stop in at the Lindell and talk with the stage agent Randall. He might have just the investment you are looking for."

Jason looked over James's shoulder at Jim and said, "Let me know when the baby arrives."

Jason left the buggy and walked slowly down the street to the hotel. He took the time to wrap his mind around the possibility of investing in a stage line with Randall. His arrival in St. Louis had coincided with Randall's departure, but James had filled him in on the idea of investing in a line that could operate on its own even after the railroad was completed. Randall would now have the information they needed to choose the right location. Jason had seen the growth in certain areas west and knew he liked the run from Colorado Springs to Denver. The train would come into Denver, but folks would still need to get to the Springs.

If Denver continued to grow as fast as St. Louis, it would surely support a passenger and a freight service to Colorado Springs. Jason was also pleased that this had worked out, where he could get this started before he left for another trip to Denver. He intended to make Jim's newborn child the beneficiary of anything he made if he died. Randall found this part of the contract a little strange, but he did know the dangers Jason would face riding security on the freight lines for two more years.

The meeting went better than anticipated; Randall agreed with his choice of line and added another to the deal that he thought would be just as lucrative. They shook hands, and Randall started the process of buying out the home office. He told Jason the contracts should be complete before he left for Denver. Everything was flowing in the right direction for Jason's return to West Virginia.

The next evening, he had dinner with Jim and Alice, James, and a very healthy baby boy named John Jason, who slept through the entire celebration. Jason was honored that they had given his name to their first born. Jim said if it hadn't been for John and Jason, he would have never made it home. James was pleased as well; he thought there were enough Jameses; Jim was the fifth generation, and besides, there would be other boys.

CHAPTER FIFTY

Jason

Four days later, Long Rifle climbed onto the top of a freight wagon and left for his second run to Denver. Jason had invested all his earnings from the first run and his estimated earnings from his second run into the newly formed Randall-Jason stage line. Randall would be overseeing the setup and equipment purchases, and by the time he reached Denver, it should be operating. Randall could be there by train ahead of the freighters. Even though he knew the risks, Jason had faith in Randall's knowledge of the business. James and Jim were kidding him about becoming a rich businessman. Jason liked the sound of *businessman* compared to *sharpshooter*.

He took more pride in his ability with a rifle now that he was using it to save lives, but he also knew the possibility of a necessary kill was never far away. Taking a life did things to your soul, whether it was justified or not.

The endless confrontation between Indian and settler was always worse in the spring of the year. During the spring, the young braves had time on their hands. Raiding other tribes, their longtime enemy, and the settlers was a way to pass the time. Small bands of nonreservation Indians continued to acerbate the problems on the trail for the freighters as well as the immigrants. Jason had to be vigilante but stayed hopelessly optimistic that his presence protected the long line of wagons.

HOME

On their approach to Pawnee Rock, they were greeted by a group of about twelve Indians. Red talked with them in their language, some of which Jason could understand. They told Red the Rock was occupied by several families who intended to stay. The Indians were unhappy that they were building homes on their summer grounds. Red asked them if they would compromise and let the settlers build on the lower branch of the creek. They agreed to talk about it with their leaders, and Red promised he would persuade the settlers to wait for an agreement. Jason was sure none of this would save the Indians' ground in the long run.

Red agreed, but even though legally he had no control of such matters, he thought it was worth a try. It would also mean a comfortable stop over for the wagons and could mean some freight deliveries for the builders. Jason had never thought of Red as a businessman until that moment. He had arranged a compromise that helped Indians by defusing their anger, the whites establish farms, and his father's freight line.

Red arranged a sit-down for the two parties, and the farm town at Pawnee Rock was established on the lower branch of the creek by the Browns' and the Thomases'. Jason met both families; they were ready to settle and thought being neighbors with reasonable Indians would be a perfect situation. They planned to build cabins and a church. After talking with Red, plans for adding a general store were drawn up. Red made arrangement for a shipment of lumber on the freight lines return from Denver.

"Red, was this something you already had on your mind?"

"I've been thinking on what to do after the railroad takes over the long hauls. This looked like a chance to establish a depot." Then he paused and smiled at Jason. "What, you thought you were the only one thinking about a future?"

"I'm new to business. My investment is to raise capital to go home with but you. You're a visionary."

"I don't know about that, but it feels good to think I could settle down."

CHAPTER FIFTY-ONE

Randall and Jason

Jason found himself in Denver when his contract was fulfilled; it was January of 1867. The Randall-Jason Denver stage line was operating at a huge profit. His investment had paid off better than anyone had predicted. The second stage line that he and Randall owned was struggling. Randall asked if Jason would work on the line for a while before he left. Jason agreed to work as a security detail, but no one was to know that he was an owner. Randall thought that he might be able to help solve the line's issues in that capacity. He expected it was an employee problem but had been unable to verify. The line was operating at capacity according to the books but losing money systematically. If it was carrying the number of passengers on the booking lists, there shouldn't be any losses.

 Jason arrived in the town of Shawnee and checked into the only hotel. For several weeks, he watched the stage come and go, and when the opportunity arose, he interviewed some passengers. With most of the runs, the passengers seemed to be satisfied customers, but about every fifth run, the stage was without passengers when it arrived in Shawnee. Jason wondered why these runs were traveling empty. These coaches didn't off-load any mail or other cargo either. It was not profitable to drive an empty stage even on a short run.

 The return trip had cargo and passengers bound for Colorado Springs. A round trip took two days, departing in the morning at a reasonable hour and arriving just before super if the coach had no breakdowns. It was always a little faster coming into Shawnee since the town was a lower elevation than Colorado Springs. There was a brief stop about halfway where passengers stretched their legs and could get a bite to eat. The stage stop did not belong to the Randall-Jason line, but it was a convenient and a well-run establishment.

Randall had set up a schedule where the drivers alternated daily, so the drivers were always well rested. Security details or men who rode shotgun could do as many as three entire routes without a break. Jason found out that most of the security guys were ex-soldiers and preferred to layover in Colorado Springs, where there was more to do for entertainment. Some of them would take a run to Denver occasionally. Randall had allowed the security details a little more leeway simply because of the stress involved with protecting the more valuable shipments or payroll boxes. He could assign them according to their ability with a rifle and their negotiation skills. Randall told Jason that the "shotguns" were more likely to quit without notice, just not as reliable as the drivers.

Apparently, over the last couple of months, two of these guys had simply walked off the job in the middle of a run. The driver said when they stopped at the midway point, they disappeared. Randall inquired in the café, and he was told they each bought a horse and rode out the back. The driver told Randall the one fellow was unreliable, made him nervous, and would drink while on the coach, so his disappearance hadn't been a surprise or even a bother. The man he knew as Johnson was an entirely different matter, but he had also just ridden away according to the shopkeepers.

Jason found both disappearances disturbing. If you were going to quit your job, why not wait until the end of the line and collect your pay? It didn't make sense to walk away without provocation. He did note that in both instances, it was on a trip to Shawnee and with the same driver. It bothered him enough that he had Randall check with the home offices about any previous incidents of people disappearing on this stretch of the stage line.

After talking with Randall, Jason rode the stage to Colorado Springs as a passenger and began his surveillance there. Just like in Shawnee, the stages would come and go filled with passengers and mail. The fifth coach would leave empty. He suspected since it wasn't the same day of the week, no one in the office had noticed. Jason did notice that these coaches were always driven by the same driver, and no guards were in place when they left the depot. He had no way of knowing why the security details weren't on these runs.

Jason started riding along as extra security on any of the runs that had valuable cargo on board. No one questioned Randall assigning an extra man with gun skills to the payroll runs. Jason was delighted with the change in pace from the slow-going oxen wagons of the freight company. A stage coach ride could be exciting depending on the driver and the weather conditions. He discovered quickly that the ride atop of the coach on a dry day was much more pleasant than cooped up inside, surrounded by mail and knee to knee with strangers. Whether you rode up or down, the next aspect was the condition of the road. The run from Shawnee to Colorado Springs was on a well-maintained road; as long as it was a sunny day, it could be quite enjoyable.

Randall and Jason manipulated the driver schedule and the security detail so that his next run would be on an empty run.

When he arrived at the depot, ready for the stage ride, the depot officer said, "We don't need your services today."

"Why not?" Jason asked, pretending surprise.

"No cargo."

"Well, I need to get to Shawnee, so I'll just ride along if that's okay," Jason said flatly.

"Suit yourself," the station master responded. "You get paid either way." And then he disappeared into the back of the office. A few minutes later, the driver emerged from the back; he looked angry but didn't say anything.

Jason extended his hand and said, "Glad to meet you, I'm—"

Before he could finish the driver said, "I know who you are, you and your rifle."

It wasn't the response Jason was expecting. It meant his cover was blown. He quickly pulled from his Secret Service training and came up with a credible lie.

"My name is Sam. This is Long Rifle's gun. He gave it to me when he finished his freight contract."

The driver visibly relaxed, and his anger seemed to subside.

"You know, the company will never know if you sit this ride out."

"I get it, but I have a reason to go to Shawnee."

"Does she have long legs and a great smile?" the driver asked.

"I think she's the one I promised I'd be back today."

"Okay, Sam, if you insist."

They climbed aboard the empty stage and thundered out of town. They hadn't gone very far when the driver veered off the main road and started up a slight incline.

"What's up?"

"Shortcut, I don't do it with passengers. It's a little rougher, but it saves time."

Jason immediately went into observation mode; this didn't feel right. A hundred feet farther, the road passed between two cliffs; he thought he saw movement on the top. He leaned into the driver and said, "There's a man on that cliff."

The driver made no response and allowed the horses to slow down through the pass. The two men were on Jason before he had a chance to react. They tossed him off the stage, and one held him down while the other beat him. Before Jason passed out, he was aware that the driver sat on the stage and watched.

He could hear the discussion but was only understanding some of what was said. They were trying to decide what they would do with him, but first they needed to load the girls. Jason tried to shake the cobwebs from his head without letting on that he was conscious. He stayed facedown in the dirt, and from ground level, he watched six young women shuffle by; they were bound together.

The driver noticed that he was watching and thrashed him in the head with his own rifle. They must have assumed he was dead because the next time he came to, they were gone. Jason assessed his situation. He was a least fifteen miles from town or water. He was having trouble staying awake. His left shoulder was dislocated, and his right ankle would not bear his weight without abject pain. He needed a reason to survive, so he let himself drift to the memories of Carey that had saved him during the war. He promised her again that he would come home.

In what seemed like an instant, Jason opened his eyes and wasn't sure where he was. It was a cave not unlike the one he had lived in during the war. Two Indian men were watching him closely. He tried to move his shoulder; it was painful but functional. His ankle throbbed but was wrapped in a cooling poultice of some kind. His head was clearer but pounding. One of the Indians offered him some tea and said something in Osage that Jason could almost understand.

"Thank you," he responded, one of the few Osage words he could pronounce.

The second Indian began to fire off questions too fast for him to understand.

The older Indian took the other by his hand and said, "You must speak slowly. He does not understand."

Jason smiled and tried to respond. He did understand that they were looking for the two Indian girls whom he had seen with the outlaws. When he had watched the women shuffle by, two of them wore moccasins. Between the English they knew and the Osage Jason knew, they pieced together the story. The stage line was being used to ship these captured girls to the way station, where they were exchanged for money and sold to the comancheros, who then shipped them to points west and south to Mexico, where they would be lost forever. The younger of the two Indians was their father.

Jason knew the only chance of saving the girls was to get to the way station before the transfer took place. He explained to the Indians where they were being taken. They knew the place, and on horseback, they could be there ahead of the stage. Jason was mounted on one of the pack horses, and the three men left immediately. They rode hard and fast and reached a place above and behind the café well ahead of the stage. They observed the station for several minutes and determined the only people around were the family that operated it.

The stage arrived while they watched. The driver escorted the girls around to a shed located behind the way station, shoving them inside with brutality. The younger Indian was poised to attack, but luckily, his father restrained him.

"Let the white man go in the front door with his rifle, and we will sneak all the girls away."

"Good plan," Jason said. "But it won't work. Look over there."

Opposite them on the rocks were the comancheros. Jason and the two Indians dropped down below the rim to be hidden and reformulated. They knew it would be tricky, but they would need to wait for the Comancheros to enter the waystation. During the negotiations, the girls could be removed from the shed. As soon as they were clear and on the run, Jason would cover their escape. The younger Indian looked at Jason with skepticism and gestured that it would take a great marksman to be accurate from the clifftop.

The older Indian said, "This is the Long Rifle of Pawnee Rock, Red's white brother. He will protect our escape."

Jason found the right spot and figured his calculations. The Indians began their descent so they would be in position when the comancheros entered the station. Jason figured the exchange would involve some haggling and drinking. He hoped that this had been going on long enough that both sides were trusting enough that the girls would not be moved until the comancheros were ready to leave. He watched through his scope and spotted the Indians entering the shed; he hoped the pioneer girls would trust the Indians enough to leave quietly. He was reassured as, almost immediately, they were filing out, moving swiftly toward cover, with one Indian in front and one behind. He repositioned his rifle in preparation. It occurred to him that any shot would have be a killing shot, and he switched himself into assassin mode but prayed that it would not become necessary. After fifteen minutes of watching the doors, Jason backed away without firing a shot. He joined the Indians; none of the girls had been harmed. They put the six girls on the ponies, double, and walked back to the cave.

The two Indians guided all six girls back to their homes. It turned out that these girls were living near the Osage camp and knew the two Indian girls well. They were living in harmony with their Indian neighbors, which was how they came to be captured together.

Jason arrived back in Shawnee in time to apprehend the unsuspecting outlaw driver. Randall had figured out the station master's role in the smuggling.

When Randall and the authorities arrived at the way station, they found the proprietors dead and the station burned to the ground. Jason and Randall did not want the Indians blamed, so they rebuilt the station and it became the property of the Randall-Jason stage line. Several bodies were found in shallow graves behind the shed where the girls were held. They suspected they were the bodies of girls who resisted and any security guys who weren't cooperative. Johnson's body was among them.

Several weeks later, Randall and Jason had dinner in the Denver establishment that had become the main arrival and departure of their stage line. Jason was departing the next morning for St. Louis; Randall was trying to talk him into staying or at least coming back.

"I want to be home forever. My plan is to make arrangements to sell my interest in the stage line."

"Why not stay involved, bring Carey west?"

"Sorry, Randall, the West Virginia mountains call to me."

"Here's to the best partner I will ever have!" They raised their glasses and enjoyed the rest of the evening without any more talk of business.

CHAPTER FIFTY-TWO

Uncle Jason and Jay

When Jason arrived in St. Louis, he was met by Jim and his young son. His namesake was almost three years old and talked nonstop from the station to the house.

Jason helped him down from the carriage, and he charged to the house, yelling, "My uncle Jason is here!"

Alice came to the door, wiping her hands on a towel, and Jason could see she was expecting. He thought of the last time he had seen Carey and thanked the good Lord for stopping him from doing what was in his mind and heart at that moment. Regardless of his future with Carey, he knew he would have lived to regret that moment. It would have been the action that would have sent his soul into eternal hell.

Alice hugged him and said, "You will stay with us for a while?"

"For a while, but I am eager to return home."

"I wish you would stay in St. Louis, but Jim has been telling me about your Carey."

Jason looked at Jim. Jim flinched a little under his gaze. He hadn't even considered how Jason would feel about his telling Alice about Carey. Initially, Jason was upset to think that his life was being casually discussed behind his back. He looked around the home that Alice had made for her family and realized that they considered him family, and it was only natural that he be a topic of discussion.

"Uncle Jason, come with me. I want to show you something," Jay demanded.

Jason found himself being dragged toward the stairs. He smiled at Jim and Alice and followed the small boy up. He scooped him up and ran two steps at a time to the top. Jay laughed, and it was one of the most soothing sounds Jason could remember.

The boy invited him into his room. Above his bed, an American flag was hanging, and in a wooden frame next to it was Jim's tattered uniform. Jason was staring at these war relics absently when Jay grabbed his hand.

"Those are just things, but tell me about these."

Jason turned to look at the box Jay held up to him. The box was packed with Indian arrowheads, spearheads, bits of colored pottery, small animal skulls, and a small gold nugget. It was quite the collection.

"So Indian stuff is your thing?"

"No, stuff from the woods. Daddy says you are a woodsman. You can teach me to track."

Jason picked up a piece of pottery and said, "You found this stuff in the woods around here?"

"Yes, Papa James takes me walking on the weekends, but he isn't a woodsman. He is a city man."

Jason smiled and thought about how Jim had wanted to learn about the woods when they met. They planned a tracking lesson for after dinner—of course, with Mom and Dad's permission.

Jay said, "Dad wants to go with us. He already said so!"

Jason smiled again. Obviously, Jim still wanted woods knowledge. They prepared for their adventure by putting together the things they needed in the woods. Jason cut each of them a tracking stick, different sizes, of course, to accommodate the two men and the small boy. Jay had his own satchel, which rested at his hip. Jim had made it from his army ammo pack, reducing it in size to work for the boy. He used it for all the things he collected on his walks. Jim gave Jay a small skinning knife in a case and explained the proper use and safety rules.

The three "men" walked through the backyard and, to Jason's amazement, into a stand of first growth trees that towered over them. Jim was pointing out some things to the boy. Jason listened and did not interject; he didn't want to interfere with the father-son bonding. He was impressed at the information that Jim was expelling. He had developed great observation skills on his own since their last discussion from the cave entrance all those years ago.

Jason stared into the great woodlands and took a deep breath of the air, and his entire being relaxed. He continued deeper into the forest and found a place where the ground had not been disturbed by anything but wild life and sat down with his back to a tree. He closed his eyes and was immediately lost in memories. When he opened his eyes, Jay and Jim had joined him in the clearing and were also seated nearby.

"We tracked you," little Jay said very quietly.

Jason was surprised at the boy's demeanor in the woods. He was so young, but apparently, his grandfather's walks had taught him a reverence for the forest. They were both looking at him expectantly, so he began lesson one in tracking woodsman style.

"Study this area within the circle of trees, and find a ground disturbance made by a deer."

Jay said, "Ground disturbance?"

Jason quickly said, "A place where you think a deer may have been."

"Oh, that's easy," Jay pointed to a track in the ground near his feet.

"That's a squirrel track," Jim said.

"Follow it, Jay," Jason said.

The boy was sharp; he followed it to the tree Jason was sitting under. When he saw it had disappeared, he looked up, and to his delight, he found the squirrel on the limb above Jason's head. The irate squirrel chattered and ran further up into the tree. The trio laughed, and Jay went back to his deer hunting. With very little difficulty, he found the first track. Jason stood up and joined Jay; Jim followed along, giving Jason the lead. After they found the next set of tracks, Jason explained how to use the tracking stick. They measured the distance between the first two tracks. Jay, on his own, continued along until he came to a log.

Jason knew the deer most likely jumped over the log, so the next track would be farther away, but the question would be in what direction. Jason sat down on the log and watched the boy and his father work out the problem. The excitement in Jay's face was worth the wait. The fact that he worked it out with the help of his father made Jason's enjoyment heighten as well.

These were the memories that kept you together later in life when things got overwhelming. His memories of the woods and learning from his father were rushing back. Jason had to bring himself back to the tracking to keep his emotions in check.

Realizing their tracking was taking them closer to their quarry, Jason touched his fingers to his lip. Total silence was now a part of their adventure. The tracks were getting fresher as they approached an opening in the trees. A beautiful meadow opened up ahead of them. The three "men" stooped down at the edge of the tree line and observed the small herd of deer.

Jay could not contain his excitement.

"Look," he said, jumping up excitedly, "that one has horns!"

All the deer's heads came up, and several does stomped their feet in anger. Then as quick as a flash, they were all gone. Jim started to reprimand the boy.

Jason touched his arm and said, "No, we didn't need meat. This was all about tracking."

Jim smiled and said nothing at all.

*****

Alice took Jay to bed, and Jim and Jason enjoyed a glass of bourbon by the fireplace. They sat in silence until she returned.

Alice joined them with a tray of coffee.

She said, "Uncle Jason has made quite the impression on our son."

"He makes my leaving even harder. I have been procrastinating. What if my home isn't my home anymore?"

Alice glanced at Jim and then said to Jason, "You must go home. The sooner you get there, the sooner you can come back."

"He won't be back anytime soon," Jim said with a sadness. "Next time we see this man, he will be introducing us to his children."

Jason stared into the fire, but he knew the answers were not there. He downed the rest of the bourbon and announced, "You are both right. I will leave in a month's time. Jay and Jim need to know enough about tracking to continue their education without me."

"Yes, then when you return, we will track and procure dinner," Jim said with a big grin.

CHAPTER FIFTY-THREE

Jason and Ethan

The month Jason spent with Jim, Alice, and Jay had passed very quickly. He sat on the train, feeling alone again. His life since the war began was a series of long periods of intense loneliness interspersed with short friendships. The only constant was Carey; he guessed, in a way, Grandmother's prediction had already come true. His entire life had revolved around Carey even though they were not together for most of it. He remembered that Daniel had been included in that prediction. He just never thought Daniel would be the one with her.

Jason had never sent the letter he had written and rewritten to Daniel. It just never seemed right, and he fluctuated between anger and guilt whenever he tried to write it. He thought he had come to terms with all of it. After spending time with Jim's son, he felt like he could be Uncle Jason to Daniel and Carey's child or children without remorse. They were innocent of all the past. God willing, they would grow up without the fears of war.

Jason had decided to travel in style on his second train ride. His first from Denver to St. Louis, he had signed on as a Pinkerton Guard. Even though Randall had found a buyer for Jason's interests in the stage line, he was not ready to spend any of his fortune on travel expenses, and technically, the deal had not been settled when he left Denver. The Pinkertons had paid him for his duties and provided him with nice accommodations. When he reached St. Louis and checked with his bank, he had received a very large bank draft.

Jason was now a rich man. His plans to return to Carey with a fortune had come through, but he was still not sure she would or could accept him back into her life.

Jason entered the impressive Royal Palace Car with its cushioned seats, white tablecloths, crystal chandeliers, and beautiful place settings. He felt out of place and started to go back to the bar, but he wasn't quick enough.

"Are you joining a party, or are you alone, sir?" asked a waiter.

"Alone," Jason answered.

"No, he is not alone," shouted a voice from a nearby table.

Jason turned; he saw the familiar but very ancient wrinkled face of Ethan Henderson.

"Bring him over here and sit him down with me, boy," came the voice that Jason remembered from their first encounter.

Jason was shocked at Ethan's appearance; he looked so old. He was not the massive man he had been six years ago.

As Jason took a seat, Ethan ordered whiskeys and said, more to the waiter than to Jason, "We need to celebrate this reunion right." Then he straightened in his seat and said to Jason, "Say something, son. You're making me nervous. You do remember me, don't ya?"

"Of course, I remember," Jason said quickly. "It's just odd seeing you here."

Ethan laughed and said, "The first time we meet, I was in a mess tent. This is just a fancy version of the same thing."

The waiter arrived with their whiskeys. Jason raised his glass and said, "It is great to see you."

Ethan smiled and raised his glass as well, and they both slammed the whiskeys down. Amid the warm glow of the drinks, they had a companionable dinner. Ethan told Jason that when the war ended, he went west and founded a gun-manufacturing company in St. Louis. He was traveling east to discuss some new designs with a financial partner in New York. It had become a regular trip for him.

Jason briefly filled him in on his story. Ethan was particularly interested in the shot that killed the deer from the riverboat. He had actually overheard the account from a man in the bar at the Lindell Hotel in St. Louis a few years back.

"Now I wish I had asked the name of the shooter. I might have believed the story if he had said Jason Emerson."

"It was that shot that helped bring me out of the hole I had crawled into after I left Washington."

"Glad to hear you found a way out of that hole I warned you." Ethan smiled and said, "Enough of the past, where are you headed now?"

Jason found himself rambling on about Jim, Alice, and Jake and finally Carey. He told Ethan the whole story. Ethan encouraged him to follow through; even a friendship and being home would heal the wounds.

"It sounds like you can always go back to St. Louis if it doesn't work out. You have a family there." Then he laughed and added, "And me."

Jason smiled at the old man. They raised their glasses, tossed down the third whiskey of the evening, and stumbled back to their sleeping compartments.

Jason was in the dining car early the next morning. Ethan came in about ten minutes later and took the seat opposite him. The two men sat in silence. As the train approached the Ohio River at Belpre, Ohio, the great arched piers of the new bridge came into view. The train cars were loaded onto a ferry and moved slowly across the river to Parkersburg. The papers said, when completed, it would be the longest railroad bridge in the world. The fifty-three massive stone arches towered above the ferry. The train conductor told Jason and Ethan they should have put their trips off for a week. They could have crossed the Ohio on the bridge; it was very near completion. Then a passenger could travel from St. Louis to New Jersey without getting off the train. Jason didn't say so, but he was pleased to be on the river instead of the bridge.

He watched the train pull away from the river. He waved over his shoulder to Ethan, who stood in the door of the dining car. Jason never saw Ethan again. He stepped off the ferry and he was in West Virginia. His home was less than a day's ride away. He needed a horse, so he headed for the livery stables recommended by the train porter.

CHAPTER FIFTY-FOUR

Jason and Em

He quickly picked a plain brown gelding; its only distinction was it carried an army brand, "US." The proprietor said the horse had been at Gettysburg. He was a veteran, abandoned by his owner, who had taken the train west. Jason paid more than he thought he should, but the horse came with a complete set of tack and a quiet, melancholy look. He could be heading out of town within the hour.

He picked up supplies and left Parkersburg on the same road he and Jim had traveled all those years earlier. He left the main road and started cross-country through the woods in as straight a line as possible toward the cove farm that he had walked away from on the way to war. Traveling in the woods, using skills that he thought he had lost, was somehow relaxing. He slowed his pace and took in the scenery. His green mountains were close enough to see.

He kept Spruce Knob in sight and found the old trail over the top that would bring him down to the trace above the cabin. He camped along the way. Even though he wasn't sure of what would transpire, being back in his mountains convinced him he was supposed to be home. He reached the mountain ridgetop; the view from the top, rows and rows of the deep-blue mountains stretching as far as he could see, made him dizzy; he was home.

The next portion of the trail took him into the mountain meadow; it was dotted with sheep. It was a large flock. They were all fat and healthy looking. A large white dog was circling them slowly but seemed to be the only shepherd in attendance. The dog stopped when he saw the man on the horse then continued, accepting that Jason was not a threat. Jason skirted along the edge of the meadow so he would not disturb the flock. A few raised their heads and returned to their grazing as he passed.

Jason was reminded of Carey's dreams of raising sheep on their farm. It looked like with Daniel's help, she had realized her dream. Her farm was the only one near enough to use this meadow for pasture. Jason decided arriving unannounced at the cabin would be too awkward. He changed his course and started toward town. He hadn't gone very far on the creek road when he found himself drawn into the woods. He dismounted and led his horse through the trees near the creek. As he entered the clearing surrounding the tree, he saw the figure of a small girl sitting at the base of the tree. It was Carey, but it couldn't be; Jason blinked and rubbed his eyes.

The small figure jumped up, but she was not startled.

Em said, in a very clear voice, "I have been waiting for you."

Jason stood speechless and a little frightened. He must be having a vision.

"I'm Catherine Emerson Sawyer, and I have been waiting for you."

"I don't understand. No one knew I was coming home."

"I did. My grandmother told me."

"You have your grandmother's gift?" Jason asked.

"Yes," Em responded. "And my mother said you promised to come home."

"What about your father?"

"My father is dead."

"Daniel is gone?"

"Over a year ago. That's when I saw you coming. Now let me take you home. Mother is waiting."

Jason started to object, but when this small child took his hand, he knew this was how it was supposed to be. She led him through the woods to the creek and up the hill to the cabin he had built. The dogs greeted him in the yard as if he had just been gone for the day. Carey waited on the porch. The last of the darkness from the war faded from his heart, and he was home.

ABOUT THE AUTHOR

M. L. Gallagher grew up in the mountains of West Virginia. She was drawn to the Civil War history of the area from a young age.

While riding horses in the Highlands of North Carolina with some friends, she came upon a pre–Civil War cabin nestled on a mountain farm. The local historians said the young soldier who had built the cabin came home from war, found his wife with another man, killed them, and was never seen again. *Home* is an alternate tale inspired by this tragic story.

M. L. Gallagher is also the author of *After Fallin'*, an illustrated series of short stories about falling from horseback.

CPSIA information can be obtained
at www.ICGtesting.com
Printed in the USA
LVHW080330051118
595963LV00013B/323/P